hot
summer
nights

hot summer nights

LuAnn McLane

NEW AMERICAN LIBRARY

New American Library
Published by New American Library, a division of
Penguin Group (USA) Inc., 375 Hudson Street,
New York, New York 10014, U.S.A.
Penguin Books Ltd, 80 Strand,
London WC2R 0RL, England
Penguin Books Australia Ltd, 250 Camberwell Road,
Camberwell, Victoria 3124, Australia
Penguin Books Canada Ltd, 10 Alcorn Avenue,
Toronto, Ontario, Canada M4V 3B2
Penguin Books (NZ), cnr Airborne and Rosedale Roads,
Albany, Auckland 1310, New Zealand

Penguin Books Ltd, Registered Offices:
80 Strand, London WC2R 0RL, England

First published by New American Library,
a division of Penguin Group (USA) Inc.

First Printing, August 2004
10 9 8 7 6 5 4 3 2 1

Copyright © LuAnn McLane, 2004
All rights reserved

 REGISTERED TRADEMARK—MARCA REGISTRADA

LIBRARY OF CONGRESS CATALOGING-IN-PUBLICATION DATA:

McLane, LuAnn.
    Hot summer nights / LuAnn McLane.
        p. cm.
    ISBN 0-451-21316-5 (trade pbk.)
    1. Women school principals—Fiction. 2. High school teachers—Fiction. 3. Women
teachers—Fiction. 4. Sports stories, American. 5. Love stories, American. 6. Ath-
letes—Fiction. I. Title.
    PS3613.C5685H68 2004
    813'.6—dc22   2004006688

Set in Sabon
Designed by Ginger Legato

Printed in the United States of America

BOOKS ARE AVAILABLE AT QUANTITY DISCOUNTS WHEN USED TO PRO-
MOTE PRODUCTS OR SERVICES. FOR INFORMATION PLEASE WRITE TO PRE-
MIUM MARKETING DIVISION, PENGUIN GROUP (USA) INC., 375 HUDSON
STREET, NEW YORK, NEW YORK 10014.

*This book is for Jade, Josey, Katie, Sallie,
and Halley, my "Woo Woo" sisters and
Sweet Potato Queen wannabes.
Your friendship means the world to me.*

acknowledgments

I want to give a very special thanks to the Florence Freedom professional baseball team, especially General Manager, Connie Hildebrant, and Marketing Director, Erin England. "Romance Night" at the ballpark rocked. I'm so glad you made Florence, Kentucky, your home field. Baseball, hot dogs, and romance . . . what more could a girl want?

I also want to thank Anne Bohner, my editor at NAL. You have been an absolute joy to work with.

And finally, I want to give a heartfelt thanks to my agent, Jenny Bent. Your instincts for this business are spot on. I'm so lucky to have you in my corner!

contents

hot
august
night

❧ chapter
one

Erin O'Shea blew a damp tendril from her forehead and shook her head. "Look, Dan, I know you're the athletic director, and Michael Manning is your friend, but I don't think he's the right guy to coach our school baseball team."

"He pitched major-league baseball for five years. You're not going to get anyone more qualified."

Erin placed the palms of her hands on her desk and leaned forward. "He's too high profile for our small school."

"Come on, Erin. He's been out of the majors for two years. Yeah, he's still famous, but after the initial excitement dies down, he'll blend right in."

Erin gave a short laugh that was almost a snort. "Believe me, Michael Manning *never* blends in." She tapped the metal desk with her fingernail. "If I'd been principal of Sander's High back when Michael went here, I'd have expelled his butt."

Dan tugged at his gray coach's shorts, which hugged his big belly. "Oh, yeah, you went to school here with him, didn't you?"

Erin pursed her lips and pushed back from her desk. "He was two years ahead of me, but I remember his antics well. The only reason he didn't get kicked out was because he was Reverend Manning's son and an ace pitcher to boot."

Dan removed his battered baseball cap and scratched his almost bald head. "Aw, come on, Erin. I was the varsity coach back then. Michael was just a pop-off." He chuckled. "He just had to prove he wasn't a goody-two-shoes preacher's son."

Erin's eyebrows shot up. "*Goody-two-shoes* and *Michael Manning* don't belong in the same sentence."

Dan placed the cap back on his head slightly crookedly. "Aw, he loved pranks, but he was a good kid."

Erin reached over and straightened the bill on his cap and wrinkled her nose. "You really should wash that thing. Anyway, his pranks were a little over-the-top. I remember when he ran stark naked through the sprinkler system on the baseball field."

Dan had the nerve to laugh. "You witnessed that? I thought they never could prove it was him."

"I saw him streaking as I walked to my car." Erin could have kicked herself for using *that* example, especially when there were so many to choose from. The memory caused heat to creep up her neck to her cheeks.

She turned from Dan's gaze and opened the window behind her desk wider in an attempt to cool down the stuffy office and her warm face. Oh, it had been Michael all right. When he was about to get caught, he had hopped in the front seat of *her* car. Twelve years later, the memory of all six feet four inches of his gorgeous, dripping wet body crouched down in the bucket seat of her Mustang still caused her heart to accelerate.

"Aw, Erin, he was harmless."

Her hands tightened on the window latch as she thought, *Harmless?* She swallowed as the vivid memory replayed in her mind. . . .

"Come on, Red," eighteen-year-old Michael had pleaded, wearing nothing but a ball cap turned backwards and a wicked grin. "Get me out of here. Quick!"

Of course she had complied. Girls back then had done whatever Michael had requested of them, and probably still did. At sixteen, Erin had flaming red hair, freckles, and braces. Not exactly *his* cheerleader type. Except for when she watched him pitch baseball, that breathless encounter was as close to Michael Manning as she had ever gotten, and she planned to keep it that way.

Erin turned from the window and said firmly, "We're not hiring him, Dan."

"He needs this job."

Erin rolled her green eyes. "Oh, come on. He made millions in the majors, not to mention the endorsements he had."

Dan shook his head. "Money isn't everything. Just between you and me, he's had some hard times. After the car wreck that broke his leg and crushed his ankle, he was told he'd never walk again. When I went to visit him after the accident, he promised me he'd not only walk, but he'd pitch again." Dan took off his cap and slapped it against his leg. "Damn, but that boy tried! Three operations and countless painful hours of rehab." He slowly shook his head. "It was no use. His arm was strong as ever, but his leg just couldn't support him. His career was over and it just about killed him."

"I heard he was into drugs," Erin said softly.

Dan's head snapped up. "It wasn't like that, Erin. He got hooked on painkillers, but he's over that."

Erin held up her hands. "Hey, I'm the school principal. I've got to be careful. Ask questions."

Dan blew out a breath. "I know." He wiped the sweat from his brow. "Damn, it's hot in here."

Erin gave a smile of apology. "I can't run the air in the summer when school's out. Listen, I'm sorry about Michael's bad luck, but I just don't see him fitting in here. Surely he could find a job coaching on a higher level than little old Sander's High, anyway."

Dan shrugged. "Probably. But he wants to move back home to be near his family. And as you mentioned, money isn't an issue."

Erin frowned. "There were rumors that he didn't get along with his father."

Dan angled his head at her. "He doesn't, but he adores his sister Rachel. She and her husband just had their first baby. He wants to spend some time with her."

"Oh, Dan, I don't know."

Dan pounced on her weakness. "So you'll grant him an interview?"

Erin closed her eyes for a second and sighed. "I suppose. When—"

"Great!" He pulled a cell phone from his back pocket and dialed. "Michael, come on up. Erin wants to speak to you. Yeah, I'm sure." He winked at Erin as he turned the phone off. "He'll be right up."

"Now?" Erin blinked at Dan in shock.

"Yes, he's on his way up from the parking lot."

"No! Call him back! I can't conduct an interview right now! I've been cleaning!" She threw up her hands and gazed down at her frayed jean shorts and smudged white T-shirt. "Just look at me!"

A deep, smooth voice drew her attention. "I think you look just fine." Michael Manning stood in the doorway, casually leaning one shoulder against the wooden frame. He wore gray dress pants and a white oxford shirt open at the throat and rolled up at the sleeves. A heavy gold watch, a Rolex, no doubt, encircled his left wrist, and a huge World Series ring glinted in the sunlight streaming through the window. Fit in here? Yeah, right. Erin shot a glare at Dan, who gave her a sheepish shrug.

"I've got to go." Dan turned, gave Michael a grin, and said, "And turn on the sprinklers."

Erin gasped at Dan's comment and tried to disguise it with a cough. Michael gave her a quizzical tilt of his head and Erin prayed he didn't remember her involvement in his sprinkler escapade. Surely he didn't. Except for that incident, she had been invisible to him in high school, and she looked totally different now.

But he didn't. Erin swallowed when he took two long strides into the office. *Oh . . . ,* she immediately amended that thought. He looked *better*. The same dark, wavy hair curled over his collar. His eyes were still the same intense green that had stared down many a nervous batter. The wicked grin that turned girls to mush was definitely the same. . . .

But the long, gangly teenage boy had filled out into a hard-bodied man.

"I'll leave you two to your discussion," Dan commented, and headed for the door.

Erin shot him another killer look. "You're the athletic director. You should stay."

"Michael and I have already talked. You know how I feel, Erin. The rest is up to you. You're the boss." He tipped his grungy ball cap at her and left the room.

Michael gave her a hotshot grin. "If you had been the boss when I went here, I wouldn't have hated all the hours I spent in this very office. Old Mr. Gaines sure didn't look like you."

Erin's chin came up a notch. "I think it's best if we keep our interview on a professional level, Mr. Manning," she managed in a nearly level voice. He might be big-city making her feel like the country mouse, but she'd be damned if she'd let it show. Folding her hands, she tried to appear professional in her frayed shorts and T-shirt. It didn't help that at five feet four, she had to tilt her head way back to meet his eyes.

"Point taken." With a glint in those green eyes, he leaned forward, brought his hand up to her face, and slowly rubbed the rough pad of his thumb across her cheek.

Erin took a step back and came up to the hard edge of her desk. "What are you doing?"

"You had a smudge of dirt on your cheek."

"Oh." Her hand came to her cheek, which still tingled from his touch. "I was cleaning out some files."

He grinned. "Did you find a big fat one on me?"

Erin had to laugh and suddenly felt more at ease. "We could look, but do you really think you want me to right now?"

"That probably wouldn't be a good idea."

Erin cocked an eyebrow at him and nodded. "Thought so." She gestured toward a chair. "Have a seat, Mr. Manning." She sat down at her desk and felt a little more in her element. "Now, tell me why you should be the new varsity baseball coach at Sander's High."

chapter two

"Thanks." Michael was glad to sit down. The stairs up to the office had taken a toll on his leg, which was beginning to ache. He had refused to use his cane, not wanting to enter her office looking like a damned old man. He sat there for a moment, hoping to choose his words carefully, and was embarrassed to feel a drop of sweat roll from his temple and down his cheek.

"I'm sorry it's so hot in here. We don't run the air-conditioning during summer break."

"I can take the heat," he said with a cockiness he didn't feel.

She leaned forward with her elbows on the desk. "I'm sure you can. Now, why do you want to coach high school baseball? We can't offer you much money and surely you must feel overqualified."

Michael blew out a long breath and decided to cut through the crap and be honest. "This wasn't my idea.

My sister Rachel saw the ad in the paper and called me." He shook his head. "After I finally realized that my pitching career was over, I wanted to stay as far away from baseball as I could."

"So why are you here?"

"Because Dan and Rachel double-teamed me. Talked me into it."

"Mr. Manning—"

Michael held up a hand. "No, wait. I was all set to humor them just to get them off my back, but while I was waiting for Dan to call me up here, I went over to the ball field." Michael looked down at the floor, waiting while unwanted emotion clogged his throat.

"And?" she prompted softly.

"I still love the fucking game." Oh, shit. He hadn't meant to say *that*. He looked up into her widened green eyes . . . and felt a tug on his memory. There was something about those eyes . . . *oh, yeah.* He remembered her now. The nameplate on her desk confirmed it. "Erin O'Shea."

"I'm sorry. I forgot to introduce myself."

He grinned. "No need. I remember you. You saved my ass once."

She blushed but held his gaze. "Your bare ass."

Michael chuckled. "Yeah." He angled his head and couldn't help but stare. "You've . . . changed."

She turned a little pinker and shrugged her slim shoulders. "The braces are gone and I toned down my natural flaming red hair."

"Yeah," he replied stupidly, but this was sort of a sudden shock. He remembered a mere stick of a girl all teeth and eyes and hair who used to come to the games with her dad and yell like hell at the umps. His gaze was drawn to her full breasts nicely outlined in the T-shirt. He didn't remember *those*.

"I was a late bloomer," she said dryly.

Michael tore his gaze from her breasts and halted his thoughts of what they must look like naked. Her cheeks were now redder than her hair and he realized he was royally screwing up the interview. "Sorry, I guess we got kind of off the subject."

"Yes, Mr. Manning, we did."

Michael cleared his throat and wondered why in the hell he was so damned nervous. He had pitched a shutout in the seventh game of the World Series, been the host of *Saturday Night Live*, for God's sake. Why was one small female making him so skittish?

Because those glory days were over and he was reduced to *this*. He suddenly wanted out of there. Now. Sweat trickled down his back, making his shirt stick to his damp skin. Damn his sister Rachel for talking him into this.

"You were saying," she prompted with a slight frown, "that you still loved the game."

"Yeah, I do," he admitted, and forced himself to go on. "Dan was the reason I made it to the majors. Winning the state championship was in a lot of ways more exciting than winning the World Series. Sander's High hasn't had a state championship team since, and I'd like to change that."

"You think you could bring us a state championship?"

Ah, he had her interest now. The fact that she so clearly didn't want to hire him brought the competitive spirit that had been buried for almost three years. "Damn straight. I know the game inside out. I want to start working with the pitching staff, and Dan said your summer baseball camp starts next week. I know it brings the school athletic money, and without a coach, you can't run the camp."

"Dan said he'd fill in."

"I'll have the camp full."

She shook her head. "I can't offer you much money."

Michael leaned forward in his chair. "I want to donate my salary for a baseball scholarship." There, he just sealed the deal.

"You're making it hard to refuse you, Mr. Manning."

"Why in the world would you want to refuse me?"

She hesitated. "I hate to bring this up, but . . . there have been . . . that is, I've heard . . ."

"Spit it out." He leaned back and felt his spirit deflate.

"That you've been involved with drugs."

Michael felt a flash of white-hot anger. "That part of my life is over." He pushed up to his feet, ignoring the pain in his stiff leg. "And so is this interview."

She stood as well. "Mr. Manning, wait!"

"Give Dan my regrets, Miss O'Shea." Gritting his teeth, he headed for the door and prayed that his leg would get him down the stairs.

Erin came around her desk and caught up with him in the hallway. "Please." She put a restraining hand on his arm and felt the tension in his hard muscle. "I didn't mean to offend you. As principal of this school, I have to be careful."

"My past isn't the prettiest, as I'm sure you well know, but it's who I am." He gripped the banister. "I'm not about to apologize or answer for it. Not to you or to anyone." With a dismissive wave of his hand, he began a halting descent. "Find yourself another coach."

Erin watched his painful progress, wanting to go after him, to offer him her apology and a shoulder to lean on. But she knew male pride when she saw it and refrained.

At one point, though, near the bottom of the steps, he stumbled when his leg seemed to give out. Her hand flew to her mouth. She took a step down when he paused as if he couldn't go on. "Do you need some help?"

He turned and gave her a not-on-your-life glare. "I'm fine."

It was obvious he was lying, but she turned away. But instead of going back to her office, she went into a classroom that overlooked the baseball field and back parking lot. Erin waited by the window until she saw him exit the building and limp toward a sleek black sports car. He paused, though, and leaned his tall frame against the chain-link fence of the baseball field backstop. For a long moment, he simply looked out over the ball field.

Erin took a deep, shaky breath as she watched him with his fingers curled in the metal fence. Was he remembering the games played on that field? She had gone to almost every one with her father, and many of the away games, at first to keep him company after the untimely death of her mother when she was only thirteen. Baseball had given Erin, a quiet, geeky teenager, the freedom to yell, to cheer, to blow off steam in the stands, but mostly to grow closer to her gruff father, who found it difficult to show emotion. The pure love of the game had been their connection, a way of coping with his losing his wife, and her losing her mother. To this day, they still went to games together.

Ahhh, and watching Michael pitch had been pure pleasure. Her father had called him "poetry in motion with a cocky edge." At thirteen, Erin had been happy to get the chance to stare at Michael. He had been her first crush . . . hers and every other girl's in Sander's City. Of course, he probably didn't realize she had been in the stands, cheering until her voice became hoarse.

When Michael finally walked slowly over to his car, she was relieved to see the limp had improved. He folded his tall frame into the low-slung car and roared away, spitting gravel and creating a cloud of dust in a show of typical male anger.

Erin closed her eyes and felt tears burn behind her eyelids. She and her father had followed Michael's career through college, the minor leagues, and his swift rise to the majors. How hard it must have been to reach his dream only to have it taken away in an instant. She leaned her forehead against the cool windowpane with a heartfelt sigh.

"Erin, what happened?" Dan asked as he entered the classroom. "I just saw Michael speed out of the parking lot like a bat outta hell."

Erin swallowed the lump rising in her throat. "I

ticked him off." She turned and looked at Dan. "I was about to offer him the job, but I had to ask about the drug thing."

"Aw, damn. Erin, I told you that was over."

"Dan, I had to! I'm responsible for these kids!"

Dan took a deep breath. "Erin, the only drugs he ever messed with was goddamned painkillers. That boy was so determined to make it back to the majors that he ended up doing more damage to his leg." Dan pounded his fist in his hand. "He was under so much pressure. Yeah, he got hooked on pills and hit a real low there for a while, but he's on the mend."

"Dan, I'm so sorry."

Dan adjusted the bill on his cap. "It's not your fault. Rachel and I pushed Michael into this, and I didn't give you fair warning."

"Do you have his address?"

"You gonna talk to him?"

Erin nodded. "His leg is really messed up, isn't it?"

"Yep, but the pity of it all is that his arm is as strong as ever."

Erin remembered the power she had felt when she grabbed his arm. "What a shame."

Dan nodded. "I know you love the game. You used to ride those umpires alongside your daddy. Quiet little thing like you! I used to get a kick out of you at the games."

"Now that I'm principal, I have to bite my tongue."

"How's your daddy been?"

"Crotchety as ever," she said with fondness.

"He'd sure love to see a championship team at Sander's High."

"Dan, you're not playing fair."

Dan shrugged his meaty shoulders and then scratched Michael's address on a piece of paper. "He's renting his sister's condo in that big complex overlooking the lake. Swing around towards the back."

Erin nodded as she looked at the address. "I know where that is."

"Erin?"

"Yes?" She pocketed the note and gave Dan her attention.

"You know how much I care about this school and these kids. I would never ask you to hire someone who would do any harm. Michael would be good for the school."

"And the school would be good for him?"

"Yeah. Damn hardheaded boy just doesn't know it."

Erin gave him a reassuring grin. "I'll just have to undo the damage I've done."

"Knowing Michael, he won't make it easy for you. You want me to come along?"

"I deal with over five hundred teenagers on a daily basis. I think I can handle one arrogant male."

✎ chapter three

Michael's body was slick with sweat, but damn, it felt good to exercise. Nothing helped to ease frustrations better than an intense workout. Clenching his teeth, he grunted his way through another set of arm curls until his biceps bulged and his arms quivered. After dropping the weights to the floor with a soft clunk, he mopped the sweat from his face with a small white towel.

He had transformed Rachel's basement into a workout center and was grateful for the hot tub off the back patio. After some ab crunches, he planned to soak his tired body in the steaming water.

Fifty sit-ups later, he decided that time had arrived. With a groan, he pushed up from the floor and guzzled a bottle of water. He stripped off his sweaty T-shirt and shorts and wrapped a towel around his waist, intending to soak in the nude. The patio had high brick walls on either side and butted up to tall trees, so privacy wasn't a problem.

Michael tossed his empty water bottle in the trash and decided he needed another to take outside with him. Leaning heavily on the banister, he headed up the stairs to the kitchen.

Just as he pulled a bottle of water out of the refrigerator, the doorbell rang. Michael winced. This was going to be Rachel wanting a full account of his interview with the little redheaded principal. "Damn woman," Michael muttered as he headed for the front door. "I should have told her to shove her job up her uptight little ass."

Michael forced a smile for his sister as he swung the door open. His smile faded and his eyes narrowed. "What in the hell are you doing here?"

"Good evening to you too, Mr. Manning," said the uptight little redhead. "May I come in?"

He gave her his most intimidating glare, the one that had made even Ken Griffey Jr. tap his bat on home plate and spit, but she seemed unaffected. Ah, a challenge. With a sweeping gesture that made his towel dip lower on his hips, he gave her a curt nod. He noticed her gaze lower and grinned inwardly when her cheeks turned pink. He perversely let the towel ride low and decided he would have some fun pushing the prim little principal to the limit until he kicked her out the door.

With a tilt of his head, he watched her lift her chin as she brushed by him into the condo. Cleaned up now, she had changed into conservative khaki shorts and a green polo shirt. Her long auburn hair was tamed with a gold clip at the base of her neck. She wore very little makeup, giving her a just scrubbed girl-next-door look that was totally at odds with her lush body.

Michael followed her into the living room and leaned an elbow on the kitchen counter that separated the two rooms. He crossed one ankle over the other and cocked a questioning eyebrow at her.

She folded her hands primly together and inclined her head in his direction. "I want to apologize for the way our interview ended and perhaps set up a time to discuss the coaching position in further detail."

"Now is fine with me."

"Mr. Manning, although I'm anxious to discuss the matter, I don't think now is the proper time." Her voice sounded cool and composed, even though he did notice she kept her green eyes carefully on his face. "Now, when would a meeting be convenient for you? My schedule is fairly open."

Michael barely resisted rolling his eyes. If she had a British accent, she'd sound like goddamned Mary Poppins. Realistically, he figured she wasn't the snotty bitch she was coming off as, and he knew it was far from her intent. But being the son of a preacher, he had grown up rebelling against all things prim and proper, and she was one of them.

"I'm ready right now." He reached with one hand and raked it through his damp hair, knowing full well it would cause a ripple of pumped-up muscle and make the towel slip an inch or so lower.

Determined to get a reaction even if it meant ditch-ing the towel, Michael reached up and casually scratched his chest. He tightened his ab muscles, showing off the six-pack he had had since high school . . . and she didn't even blink.

And then it hit him.

Aha. He wanted to snap his fingers, but that would mess up his oh-so-cool pose that was killing his leg. *High school.* She had the ugly-girl-in-high-school-turned-hot-chick-syndrome chip on her shoulder. Michael knew this because his sister had been one of them. All virginal Goody Two-shoes who hid a sensual side dying to surface, but who remained too ticked off at the guys who had ignored them as ugly ducklings to let them get within a mile. Michael frowned at Erin O'Shea and wondered if she *had* a sensual side. He was damned well going to find out.

Michael pushed away from the counter and took a step toward her. Her eyes widened a bit, but she stood her ground. "Are you ready, Miss O'Shea?"

She opened her mouth and then snapped it shut as if she didn't know quite what to say. The women he was used to would have had a flirty comeback, but she seemed at a loss. He was beginning to feel like an ass.

"Would you mind putting on some clothes, Mr. Manning?"

The uppity little lift of her chin made his sudden goodwill evaporate like summer rain on a hot sidewalk.

"Yes, I would," he all but growled. "I was about to take a long soak in my hot tub and I don't feel like putting on clothes just to take them off again." He folded his arms across his chest. "Now, are you going to offer me the coaching job or not?"

She frowned. "It's not quite that simple, we—"

"It *is* that simple." He took another step toward her, but his calf muscle chose that moment to cramp into a tight ball . . . and his leg gave out. He fell forward, grabbing for a wingback chair, but she *had* to be the hero and lunged to catch him.

Of course she couldn't begin to support his weight, and she stumbled backwards, hit the arm of the sofa, and fell. With a little shriek she took him with her and landed against the soft cushions.

"Are you okay?" Her voice was muffled behind the wide wall of hairy chest flattened against her face.

"I guess I should be asking you that." His attempt at humor was ruined by his hiss of pain.

Erin could feel the thud of his heart and taste the salt on his skin when she spoke. "I'm okay." He was struggling to get up, but his injured leg was the one close to the floor, and would not support his weight. "Michael, just take it easy. You're not hurting me."

"I must be crushing . . . you . . . ahh!" He grabbed at his leg.

"What can I do?" She wanted to make his pain go away.

"I've got to make it over to the hot tub to get the muscle to relax," he said through gritted teeth.

"Oh, God, I'm sorry," she mumbled against his warm skin. "You were going to do that when I got here. This is my damned fault!"

"Ooh, watch your language, Miss O'Shea," he said, and managed to chuckle.

Erin felt the rumble of his laughter against her cheek. The soft hair on his chest tickled her nose, and she held her breath to keep from sneezing . . . and then, out of the corner of her eye, she spotted the white towel pooled on the beige carpet. *Oh, good Lord.*

Her breath came out in a rush. Michael Manning was lying on top of her stark naked. She had a sudden, almost irresistible urge to run her hands down the sleek muscles of his back and cup her palms on his sweet ass.

"Give me a minute and I'll get up." He attempted to chuckle. "That didn't come out right."

His voice interrupted her delicious thoughts. "Okay." Her mouth moved against his skin, putting his taste on her lips, his scent in her head. *Oh, my.* Heat pooled in places that had her wanting to wrap her arms around him and run the tip of her tongue over his damp skin. She balled her hands into fists and bit her bottom lip to keep from doing just that.

She felt muscles bunch and quiver as he moved and pushed up with one hand, trying to shift some of his weight off of her. This gave her an eye-popping view of his chest, and if she lowered her eyes . . . no! She would *not* look and squeezed her eyes shut until she heard him chuckle.

"So I'm lying on top of you naked and you're falling asleep? You wound my ego, Miss O'Shea."

Erin opened her eyes and tilted her head back to see his face. Although he was attempting a grin, his dark stubbled jaw was clenched, letting her know he was still in considerable pain. "I doubt your ego is that fragile, Mr. Manning. If I push up on your chest, do you think you can lean your weight on your other leg and get up?"

He took a deep breath. "If you're game. I guess we can try."

❧ chapter
four

With her elbows bent, Erin placed her hands flat on his chest, barely resisting the urge to curl her fingers in the dark silky hair. His skin was warm, moist, smooth, stretched taut over hard, defined muscle. "Are you ready?" Her voice sounded breathless and she cleared her throat.

He took a deep breath and blew it out. "I guess."

"Okay, on the count of three. One . . . two . . . three!" Erin gave him a hard shove and he pushed up to his right knee, giving her an up close view of his very male package. "Oh, God!" She squeezed her eyes shut and felt her face flame.

"Why, thank you, I think."

"Get the towel."

"I can't reach it. Come on. You've seen me. Big deal. You're going to have to sit up, scoot from underneath me, and help me stand."

The pained irritation in his voice galvanized her

into action. Averting her eyes, she scooted, pushed up on the cushions, and then stood up.

"Now, tuck your shoulder underneath my arm and I think I can stand."

"Okay." She tucked, offering him her shoulder.

He placed one heavy arm around her. "Get ready, Red. I'm going to stand up."

Erin staggered a bit under his weight, but they managed. "Where is the hot tub?"

He sighed. "That's the tricky part. Down the stairs and out on the back patio."

"How are we going to get you down the stairs?" Erin asked as she helped him hobble to the other side of the room. They paused at the top of the steps.

"I'll hold on to the banister, and you stay under my shoulder."

"That will never work. You're too big for me to handle."

"That's what they all say." His laughter ended with a hiss of pain. "Shit, shit, *shit!* You're right. This will never work."

Erin decided she was going to get him to that hot tub come hell or high water. "Sit down."

"What?"

"I said sit down," she ordered in her best Principal O'Shea voice. "You're going down the stairs on your butt."

"No way! I'll get major rug burn in places not meant to be chafed."

Erin nibbled on the inside of her cheek for a moment. "I'll be right back."

"Like I'm going anywhere," he grumbled. "What the hell are you doing?" he called over his shoulder.

Erin came back with his towel. "Lift your butt. I'm going to wrap this around you, and then you can slide down the stairs on the towel."

"Okay," he agreed, but didn't sound happy.

Erin realized how embarrassing this must be for him and was careful not to let pity into her voice. She stepped down two steps and turned toward him with the towel in her hands. Pretending to ignore his nakedness, she slipped the towel underneath him and wrapped it over his lean hips. To make matters worse, he seemed unaffected by their nearness and his state of undress.

She, however, was not. Her fingers shook as she knotted the towel. "There," she said briskly. "Now just slide down the steps and I'll help you to the hot tub."

Michael took a deep breath and glared at her. Sweat beaded on his upper lip, not so much from the pain, but from the supreme effort to keep his dick from saluting her. Damn, first he had her beneath him on the couch, and now she was all over him tying the fucking towel while giving him orders in that stern little voice that somehow turned him on. That damned gorgeous hair of hers slipped over her shoulder and brushed against his chest, tickling and enticing him. He felt his dick stir and in a moment he was going to have a huge tent in his towel. Damn, but he didn't want to give her the satisfaction of seeing him so turned on. And God help him, he was.

"Get out of my way," he growled. As soon as she moved, he bumped on his ass down the steps. She followed and offered him her shoulder at the bottom. He would have given his left nut to be able to refuse her help. But he desperately needed to get to the hot tub to loosen up the knotted muscles in his leg, and he couldn't manage without her assistance.

Leaning heavily on her, he hobbled over to the glass door and slid it open. Thank God, the tub was hot.

Without asking, she lifted the cover and turned to him. "Lean on me while you get in."

Michael felt a muscle tick in his jaw. He was getting tired of her orders but had no choice but to comply. He ditched the towel, leaned against her slight frame as he eased into the bubbling water.

After a long sigh he said, "Thanks, I can handle it from here." He closed his eyes and leaned against the back of the tub.

"I'm not leaving, if that's what you think. What if you can't get out of there?"

Michael opened his eyes and gave her a hard stare. "The hot water always does the trick. I'll be fine. Now go."

"No." She gave him a stubborn lift of her chin. "Besides, we haven't had our discussion yet."

"There is nothing to discuss."

She frowned. "What do you mean?"

"I mean I don't want your job."

She put her hands on her hips and glared right back at him. "That's not fair."

He laughed harshly. "I've found out that life isn't always fair, Miss O'Shea." He gave her a dismissive wave of his hands and closed his eyes once more. "Now go."

"I won't leave until we discuss this!"

He heard the stomp of her foot against the brick patio and had to smile. "Fine. Go get me a beer and then join me."

"Y-you mean in the tub?"

"Damn straight."

"I don't have a swimsuit."

He shrugged. "As you've already seen, neither do I. Besides, it's getting dark and the tub is secluded. No one will care that you're naked. Leave your underwear on if it makes you happy."

"Why do I have to get into the tub?"

"Because I plan on being in here for a while and it would be easier if you would join me." He opened his eyes and looked at her. "And because you piss me off, and I feel like being an ass and making you uncomfortable."

She swallowed and looked at him for a moment. "I don't like beer."

"What?"

She raised her auburn eyebrows. "You asked for a beer and I would like something to drink as well."

Well, la-di-da. "There are soft drinks in the fridge as well."

She sighed. "Do you have any wine?"

It was his turn to raise his eyebrows. "You drink?"

Up came the stubborn chin. "On special occasions, and for me, this qualifies."

He hid his grin. "There is a nice bottle of merlot on the wine rack. Just bring two glasses and I'll share the bottle with you."

"Very well." She turned on her heel and, with a stiff

back, reentered the condo. When she was inside, he chuckled. She was a piece of work. He blew out a long sigh. The hot water was working its magic and his leg was already going from white-hot pain to a dull throb . . . and it wasn't the only thing throbbing.

His dick was rock hard and bobbing around in the bubbling water. Not that he was about to get a piece of *that* uptight ass. Little Miss Redhead would never get into the tub with him. He closed his eyes, fully expecting her never to return.

Erin stomped around the kitchen, slamming drawers as she searched for a corkscrew and muttered to herself, "Arrogant man. Of all the nerve." She eyed the front door and thought about escaping, but then realized he was probably expecting her to do just that. Well, she would show him. She would just park her bare butt right beside him in that big old hot tub and see how he liked that!

She located the wine, thumped it down on the counter, and then found two wine goblets. After uncorking the wine bottle, she grabbed the goblets and headed down the stairs.

Opening the sliding glass door was a bit of a trick with her hands full, but she managed. With her head held high, she poured the wine into the goblet and wordlessly handed it to him.

"Thank you." He couldn't quite hide his surprise, and it gave her some satisfaction and the added incentive to see this thing through.

She filled the other goblet to the brim as well, took a long swallow, and then carefully placed the bottle and goblet on the corner of the tub. With jerky movements, she removed her shoes, balled up her socks, and then pulled her green polo over her head. She unbuttoned, unzipped, and then wiggled out of her shorts.

"Leaving the underwear on?"

Erin looked over at him. He cocked an arrogant eyebrow and took a leisurely sip of wine.

Erin had spent a lifetime not doing what she really wanted to do, and not saying what she really wanted to say. And what she *really* wanted to do right here, right now, was to wipe the smug look from his too-handsome face by stripping off her underwear in the warm glow of the setting sun.

For a long moment she stood there undecided in the twilight with her heart thumping. Part of her wanted to snatch up her clothes and run like hell . . . that part being her sensible, logical brain. Oh, but the other part—the sensual side of her nature that she kept hidden—was begging for a turn. A sultry breeze lifted her damp hair and blew it around her face, sounding like a soft sigh . . . or was that her own soft sigh?

The orange ball of the sun had dipped below the horizon and cooled the temperature a bit, but it was still a hot August night. She slowly raised her head, lifting her gaze from her bare feet over to the hot tub.

As if on cue, the hum of the jets suddenly ceased and the gurgle of the bubbles stopped.

Erin met his challenging gaze and made her decision.

chapter five

Well, *hot damn,* thought Michael, and he hid a Cheshire cat grin behind his wine goblet. The prim and proper principal had a naughty side. He watched her reach for the clasp in the front of a surprisingly sexy demibra with anticipation. He was a boob guy . . . nipples, to be exact. The size of the breasts didn't matter; it was the nipples that turned him on. The thought of her nipples in his mouth . . .

Damn. She dropped her hands from her bra. Apparently she had decided to leave her cream-colored bra and pretty little panties *on.* She glanced longingly down at her clothes yet again. Well, damn again. She seemed to be having a naughty-versus-nice battle within herself. He *so* wanted naughty to win, so he goaded her with an I-knew-you'd-chicken-out grin. "Running away, are you?"

Instead of answering, she took a large gulp of wine.

"Running from a challenge isn't in my nature, Mr. Manning."

And neither is getting into a hot tub naked, he thought, and forced her hand again. "Well, good, because if you want to talk to me, you gotta get in this tub."

She took a deep breath and hoisted herself up onto the first of two steps with her underwear on, but at least she was getting in with him. Hmmm, a naughty-versus-nice compromise. He hid another grin.

"Don't knock over the wine," Michael warned as she swung her leg over the edge of the tub.

"Oh!" She turned her head at his warning and then slipped, landing in the center of the big tub with a huge splash for such a little person.

When she surfaced, coughing and sputtering, Michael made the mistake of throwing his head back while laughing.

"Why, you!" She cupped her hands into the hot water and splashed him in the face.

"Hey, you got that in my wine."

Her answer was to splash him again.

"Stop it!"

She skimmed her hand across the surface, and this time she got him while his mouth was open, making it his turn to cough and sputter.

So he splashed her back and then it was all-out war.

Shrieking, arms flailing, Erin was getting the best of him. In desperation, he lunged at her in an attempt to grab her waving arms. She sidestepped him and he landed face-first in the water. Twisting, he grabbed her around the waist when he came up for air.

With a jerk, he pulled her against him. "You little hellcat!" He was breathing hard and more turned on than he had ever been in his life.

"Let me go!" Nostrils flaring, green eyes snapping, she wiggled beneath his hold.

"Not on your life," he growled, and then bent his head and kissed her, ravaging her mouth with a hot, hungry possession that had her pushing at his chest . . . but with a sudden moan of surrender, she entwined her arms around his neck and kissed him back.

Michael slid his hands from her waist to palm her sweet ass. He lifted her up, backed up, and sat down on the hot-tub seat, still kissing her deeply. She straddled him, her fingers delving into his wet hair. Prim and proper morphed into wet and wild, and Michael couldn't get enough.

He rocked her against his raging erection and lifted her higher so he could move his mouth from her lips to her breasts. Her soaked bra was now transparent, revealing pointed nipples begging for his attention. He gladly gave it, capturing the wet silk in his mouth. He heard her gasp when he lightly tugged her nipple with his teeth and then licked, and suckled.

Arching her back, she surprised him when she held his head in her hands, offering him more, urging him on. With one swift flick of his fingers, he unhooked the bra, and her breasts spilled forward. Pink-tipped and puckered, wet and glistening in the moonlight, they were perfection. Cupping the exquisite fullness in his hands, he then rubbed the erect nipples with the rough pads of his thumbs.

"God, you're beautiful," he breathed into her ear. And meant it.

She gave him a startled look as if surprised by his statement, and that bothered him. Hadn't anyone ever told her how lovely she was? Still cupping her breasts, he kissed her mouth and her delicate chin, and then nuzzled her neck.

"You're driving me insane," he growled next to her ear and then kissed her again. She tasted like woodsy merlot and wild woman, heat and silk. Michael moved his hands from her breasts around to her back, molding her soft curves to his hard body. Rocking his erection against her, he wanted her to know just how much he wanted her.

The hot water lapped around them while steam rose, swirling in the night breeze. Despite the intense heat, Erin shivered against him and whispered in a throaty plea, "Make love to me, Michael."

Ding, ding-ding. Warning bells went off in the back of his head. She might be as hot as a firecracker right now, but in the morning she was going to somehow blame this on *him*. She nibbled on his earlobe, sending his dick a different message than his trying-to-reason brain. Her breasts rubbed against his chest and he sucked in his breath.

But Michael had been around enough women to know Erin's sexy moves were instinctive, not practiced seduction. She was caught in this surreal moment of heat and steam and if he didn't put an end to this right now, he was going to royally . . . no, make that *literally,* fuck this up.

And despite what he said, he wanted the coaching

job. Yeah, he could have a high-profile job connected with the majors, but that was never what he was all about. He loved playing the game but didn't miss the limelight, despite what people thought.

"Erin?"

"Hmm?" Her eyes were closed, her lips moist and parted. She rocked against him, causing the water to ripple and lap against the side of the tub. God, she wasn't making this easy. When he didn't, *couldn't,* answer, she splayed her hands against his chest, pushed back, and gazed down at him through heavy-lidded eyes. "What?"

"We can't do this." There, he said it.

Her eyes opened wide and he felt her thighs tighten against his. "You planned this!" She tried to scramble off of his lap, but he grabbed her around the waist.

"What?" Confusion seeped into his sex-drugged brain.

Her green eyes narrowed. "You *lured* me into this tub so you could humiliate me because I pissed you off earlier."

She pushed against his chest, but he held her easily. "You came here uninvited, Miss O'Shea."

"With the mistaken impression that I should apologize!"

She wiggled and squirmed, giving the totally wrong message to his hard dick. This being-noble thing really sucked. He let her go and she fell backwards into the tub with a splash and a very *not* prim curse. "You're fired!" she sputtered as she half climbed, half slipped, over the edge of the tub.

"You can't fire me. You never hired me!"

She stooped over and picked up her shirt, giving him a nice view of her ass. Swinging around with the shirt clutched in front of her, she glared over at him. "Fine, you're hired. *Now* you're fired."

Okay, now he was really pissed. "You can't fire me for no reason."

"Sexual harassment." Her chin came up.

"You're the boss. That's *my* line."

"What!"

"You heard me. You fired me because I wouldn't fuck you." Okay, there went the noble thing out the window.

Her chest was heaving and her eyes were wide. "I never really hired you and you know it."

He shrugged. "Okay, you wouldn't *hire* me because I wouldn't fuck you. Have it your way. See you in court."

Her mouth dropped open and he fully expected to see steam coming out of her ears. She blinked, and for a terrifying moment he thought she was going to cry. Well, hell. Tears were his weakness. If she cried, all would be lost and then he would *have* to make love to her to make her feel better, right? Surely she wasn't buying into this crazy crap anyway, was she?

She swallowed, but didn't burst into tears. Thank God. Instead, she looked around for her bra, which he spotted hanging from a bush, but he kept this information to himself. Finally, she yanked on her shirt and shorts before straightening up to face him.

"Report to Dan eight o'clock sharp tomorrow morning. Baseball camp starts on Monday. Dan will spell out the details, but camp is run pretty much the same as when you were in school here. We're just a few weeks late because we didn't have a coach." She gave him a tight little smile. "Now we do."

"Erin . . ." His anger was fading. This was ending up all . . . wrong. Why did he have the uncanny ability to have people buy into his bullshit?

"It's *Miss O'Shea*, Mr. Manning. Let's keep this professional, shall we?"

Considering her bra was dangling from a bush, her statement was almost comical, but he had the feeling that if he laughed, she would come flying in the tub at him. He carefully schooled his features before replying, "You got it, Miss O'Shea."

She nodded. "Good. Now, since I'll see to it that we don't interface again unless absolutely necessary, I'll tell you two, no, make that three things."

Michael sat up straighter in the tub. "Okay."

She held up her index finger. "One, I fully expect a state championship. We're talented, but pitching has been our weakness and I think you can fix that problem." She held up another finger. "Two, I will hold you to your earlier offer to give your salary to a baseball scholarship." She hesitated and then seemed to discard number three.

Curiosity got the best of him. "And what is number three?"

She gave him a level stare and with color high in her cheeks, she said, "You should have . . . have . . ." She hesitated and then said, "*had* me while you had the chance, because you won't get another one."

Michael took a sip of his wine as he watched her strut across the patio. He had several comebacks, but being the gentleman that he suddenly was, he let her have the parting shot. With a pained sigh he looked down at his hard-on bobbing in the water as if shaking its head in disgust. "I know, I know. I'm disappointed too. But there *will* be another chance and believe me, I'll have Miss Prim-and-Proper Principal begging for it."

He took his last sip of water-splashed wine and grinned. He was back in baseball, was living near his sister, and had found a smart, beautiful woman who was a challenge. He glanced down at his still hopeful dick. Life was finally looking . . . *up*.

⤳ chapter
six

Erin slipped inside her blue Mustang and slammed the door with a satisfying bang. She was angry with Michael, but mostly at herself for her outrageous behavior and . . . God, her *language*. There was just something about that man that made her crazy. With a shaking hand, she inserted the jangling keys, and the engine roared to life. Gripping the steering wheel, she gave herself a minute before backing out of his driveway.

"My God, what was I thinking?" she whispered, wondering what craziness had possessed her to shed her clothing and get into a hot tub with Michael Manning of all people. And then she realized that she *hadn't* been thinking. She had been feeling, needing . . . wanting the touch of his hands on her skin, the taste of his mouth. Desire had clouded her usual good judgment and she vowed not to allow it to happen again. After taking a deep breath, she eased the car into reverse and then headed for home.

Erin lived only a few minutes away in a brick Cape Cod not far from Sander's High. Charming older homes, tall trees, and a neighborhood mixed with young families and seniors were a perfect fit for her conservative lifestyle. She purchased the home last year when she was promoted to principal. It was a fixer-upper, but she didn't mind. It was hers and she loved it. While many of her students couldn't wait to get away from the small-town life, Erin never had the urge to leave Sander's City. She wondered if Michael could readapt to living in a small town, and then cursed under her breath for caring.

After parking her car in the detached garage, she unlocked her back door and entered her home with a ragged sigh. The air-conditioning took the edge off her overheated body and she reached in the fridge for a cold bottle of water. She had downed half of the contents when the ringing phone startled her. Afraid it might be *him,* she allowed the answering machine to screen the call.

"Erin, it's Dan. How'd it go with Michael?"

Erin reluctantly picked up the receiver hanging on the kitchen wall. "I hired him," she said.

"Great, great!"

Erin wrinkled her nose. "I told him to report to you at eight o'clock and iron out the details for camp."

"Okay. So the two of you made up?"

God, that made them sound so . . . intimate, like they were lovers. Her grip on the phone tightened when a vivid picture of Michael dripping wet and naked formed in her mind. She slumped down in the kitchen chair. "Not exactly. Keep that man as far away from me as possible, Dan. You can deal with him."

"Oh."

Erin felt a pang of guilt at the disappointment in his voice. "I do think he'll make a great coach and he's offered to donate his salary for a baseball scholarship."

"See, he's a good guy, Erin. You just got to get to know him a little better. Give him a chance."

Erin sighed into the phone. "Dan, we're like oil and water. I gave the man a chance and he blew it." *Thank God,* thought Erin. "I'm not about to give him another one. Keep him away from me!"

"Geez, okay."

Feeling foolish, Erin lowered her voice. "I know I'm overreacting. There's just something about him that rubs me the right way." Erin put the heel of her hand to her forehead. "*Wrong way.*" Another Freudian slip? And then another thought hit her. A fear that had her heart racing. "Dan, I need Michael Manning's phone number."

"Thought you wanted to steer clear of him."

"I do, but I forgot to tell him something very important."

"Okay."

Erin jotted down the number and dialed it as soon as she hung up with Dan.

" 'Lo."

The deep rumble of his voice sent a shiver of awareness down her spine. He sounded bed rumpled and half asleep. She pictured his bare chest and long, muscled legs entwined in the sheets. . . .

"Hello?"

The irritation in his voice snapped her wanton thoughts back to reality. Still, she hesitated, not quite knowing how to approach him with her plea.

"What is it, Miss O'Shea?"

Oh, the magic of caller identification. Erin felt herself blush and was glad he couldn't see her. "Don't you dare breathe a word of what happened tonight to anyone in this town."

He chuckled. "Now, why would I do that?"

"Because you're . . . *you.*"

"Maybe you don't know me as well as you think you do. You see, I normally don't kiss and tell, but I also don't respond well to orders."

The humor reflected in his tone sent her through the roof. "I'm telling you, if you tell a soul that I got into that damned hot tub with you, I'll . . . I'll . . ."

"Cut my balls off and feed them to me?" he offered.

"Yes!"

"Oh, another mistake, Red. You see, I don't respond well to threats either."

Erin ground her teeth together, making it difficult to speak. "What *do* you respond well to?"

"Oh, I think you already know."

She gasped. "Why, you . . . *you* . . ."

"Careful." He chuckled. "You know, you really need some anger management. I can give you a name—"

"Shut up!" Erin stood up and stomped her foot, a gesture she hadn't used since first grade and had done so twice that night. God, the man had her cursing and stomping and . . .

"Calm down, Red. I promise not to tell that I saw your nearly naked body."

And melting. Her knees turned to water and she sank down on the wooden chair.

He laughed, low and sexily, and then continued to turn her on. "I won't divulge that I tasted your soft, sweet lips. Feasted on those incredible breasts."

Erin swallowed. He thought her breasts were incredible?

"God, I'm getting hard just thinking about you. Come on over. I'm in bed and, *oh yeah*, more than ready."

Erin came to her dazed senses. "You're disgusting."

"I won't tell, but I *will* kiss."

She slammed the phone into the cradle. "Jerk!" she shouted, but the vision of him naked, willing, and more than ready stuck in her head.

And would not budge.

For the next couple of days, Erin managed to avoid him face-to-face, but just knowing he was in the school building put her senses on alert. The sight of his sleek, sexy car in the parking lot made her heart thud. Hearing his voice as he walked past her office, smelling the lingering scent of his aftershave in the hallway, were enough to drive a girl crazy.

In an effort to keep her mind off of him, Erin worked nonstop in her office, cleaning, filing, and basically puttering around. Because it was summer break, she really didn't have to be there, but once school started, she wouldn't have time to do this sort of thing.

On her hands and knees, Erin wiped a trickle of sweat from her cheek as she tightened a loose screw in the bottom of her ancient desk. Earlier, the heat in the office had been tolerable, but the afternoon sun had turned the small space into an oven.

"Whew," she said, feeling a little woozy. After this last task, Erin decided, she would go home.

"Ah, I hate to bother you, but—"

Startled, Erin rose up at the sound of Michael's deep voice and smacked her head on the desk. "Ouch!" Rubbing the top of her head, she scooted out from underneath the desk, turned, and shot him a glare.

"Sorry," he offered with a sheepish shrug, but then grinned.

Still rubbing her head, Erin pushed up to her feet . . . and the room suddenly tilted. "Oh!" She put a hand to her forehead and grabbed for the desk.

"Whoa, there." Michael wrapped his arm firmly around her waist.

Erin wanted to push away but found herself limply leaning against him.

"God, are you bleeding?" He pushed his fingers gently through her hair and she was surprised at the concern in his voice. "Just a little bump," he murmured with obvious relief.

"What are you doing?" she asked when he leaned down and lifted her up into his arms. "Put me down," she protested weakly.

"Shut up and put your arms around my neck."

"No!" She tried to push at his chest, but the room started to spin and she moaned.

"Erin, you've got heat exhaustion."

"Where are you taking me?" She tried to look up at him but couldn't lift her head from his shoulder.

"I'm taking you to the weight room. The guys worked out there this morning, so Dan turned on the air-conditioning. You need some fluids and there are sports drinks in there."

"Oh, okay." She hung on to his neck while he carried her down the stairs, but she suddenly worried about his leg. "I'm too heavy, Michael," she said, not wanting to mention his weakness. "Let me walk."

"My leg is fine, if that's what you're worrying about. I'm not going to drop you," he said tightly.

"I didn't mean to insult you," she murmured against his neck. God, he smelled good.

He chuckled, making his chest vibrate against her cheek. "Does that mean you're starting to like me a little?"

"No."

"Ah, now you've hurt my feelings." He pushed open the door to the weight room.

"Oh, that feels so good," Erin said when the cool air hit her heated skin. She chuckled weakly and said, "I bet women say that to you all the time." God, she must be loopy to have said *that*.

He sat her down gently in a padded chair. "I'm going to get you a drink. Don't you dare move."

Erin managed a slight nod as a wave of dizziness washed over her.

He shook his head at her obvious distress and hurried over to the drink machine. Through half-closed eyes, she watched him insert a dollar into the slot, only to have the machine spit it back at him. After a curse, he tried again with the same result and fished in his wallet for another dollar.

Erin grinned weakly as she watched him. For a moment she thought he was going to punch the machine. He was such a *guy*. Finally the machine took pity on him and accepted the dollar bill. A drink fell with a thump and he pulled it from the machine with a triumphant grin. With a quick twist of his wrist, he took off the cap.

"Take sips at first," he instructed, and held the bottle up to her lips.

"I can do it," she protested, but her hand shook when she accepted the cold bottle.

"Sure you can," he said dryly, and wrapped his big hand over hers, tipping the bottle slightly so she could take a drink. After letting her have a few swallows, he took the bottle from her and set it on the floor but remained kneeling next to her. "Better?"

Erin nodded and he smiled, making her heart do a little flip-flop. He had a killer smile. "Thanks, Michael," she said softly.

He angled his head and looked at her as if he wanted to say something warm and fuzzy. God, if he did, she would just melt into a puddle at his feet. It was bad enough that he managed to look sexy in gray gym shorts and a tight white tank. Throw in a sensitive caring side and she would be a goner.

ᴗ chapter
seven

The sound of his name uttered in her soft sexy voice made Michael feel as if he had just gotten the wind knocked out of him. In that moment, he knew he was falling for her . . . *hard*. He was finally getting his life back on track. He didn't need a woman to come along and screw things up. And in his experience, they always did.

And she would. Oh, he had no doubt Miss Prim and Proper Principal would be a firecracker in bed, but she was a get-married-and-have-babies type.

And he wasn't.

Was he? Lately he wasn't so sure. He adored his five-month-old niece, Brooke, and admired the loving relationship his sister Rachel and her husband had.

Suddenly irritated, Michael took a deep breath and pushed up from the floor. Maybe the heat was getting to him as well. "What the hell were you thinking, working in that oven of an office? Are you crazy?"

She blinked up at him and he hated the flash of hurt in those green eyes, but he had succeeded in breaking the spell they were falling under. Her eyes quickly narrowed and she gripped the arms of the chair.

"Don't!" he warned, knowing she was going to get up.

Of course, she didn't listen.

He caught her when she swayed.

"I'm fine," she sputtered, and tried to brush past him.

"Like hell you are!"

"Let go of me!" She tugged at his hands holding her around her waist.

"You're still unsteady. Let me drive you home."

"I'll be fine," she repeated firmly.

"You can't get behind the wheel of a car, Erin."

"I walked and I only live . . . oh . . ." Hands that were pushing at his chest were suddenly clutching his T-shirt. She leaned her forehead against him.

"That does it." He picked her up again and she didn't bother to argue. "Do you need to lock things up?"

"No, the cleaning crew is in the building."

"Cleaning crew?" he asked as he carried her. "Then why were you slaving away in your office?"

"I like to be organized," she mumbled. "Do things myself."

Michael felt an unwanted surge of protectiveness and tried to shake it. Blinking in the bright sunshine, he carried her over to his car. "I'm going to put you down. Hold on to me while I open the car door."

"Okay." She hugged her arms around his waist while he unlocked and opened the door.

"There," he said, and helped to ease her into the leather seat. After closing her door, he hurried over to the driver's side.

"Where to?"

With closed eyes, she mumbled, "Left out of the parking lot, right at the first stop sign. I'm 220 Maple Street."

"Gotcha." Within a couple of minutes, he had her home.

"Thank you," she said when he came to a stop in her driveway.

"Oh, no, you don't. I'm helping you inside, Erin, so just get over it."

"How can I refuse when you put it so nicely?"

He didn't have to carry her, but held a steady arm around her waist. She unlocked the front door with a key from her pocket and turned to dismiss him, but his glare stopped any protest she had about his coming in. He ushered her straight over to a plump floral sofa.

"Sit. Now, where is your kitchen?"

She looked up at him. "I'm fine now, really."

Michael rolled his eyes. The house was tiny. He could find the kitchen himself. He pointed at her. "Don't move."

A short hallway led to a cute little kitchen. He opened the refrigerator and found a carton of orange juice among a variety of fresh, healthy looking food. By the look of the crowded refrigerator, she liked to cook, and for some annoying reason, the thought pleased him.

"She's not your type," he mumbled irritably to himself, but could picture her in nothing but an apron, puttering around in the kitchen fixing breakfast. He shook that erotic thought as a quick search led him to neatly stocked cabinets where he located a glass. He poured the juice and headed back to the living room.

She was curled up on the sofa, her feet tucked beneath her legs while she hugged a pillow. With her long auburn hair pulled pack in a ponytail and very little makeup, she could pass for one of her students. She still looked a little pale, but better.

"Drink this juice," he ordered, and handed the small glass to her.

She wrinkled her nose and saluted him but dutifully took a sip.

"Feeling better?" He forced some gentleness into his voice.

"Yes. You really can go now, Michael. I'm sure you have better things to do than to babysit me." Pink color flooded her pale cheeks, and he realized that she was embarrassed.

"Okay. But I want you to stay put for at least an hour." He picked up the remote and turned the television on. "Watch some soaps."

She shook her head. "I don't watch that stuff."

He grinned. "You don't know what you're missing."

Her eyebrows shot up. "You watch soap operas?"

"Weeks in a hospital bed after three operations will do that to ya." He watched her eyes go to his leg and then she frowned. Long red scars from lots of stitches were glaringly visible against his otherwise tan leg.

He turned away from her sympathy. "Ah, one of my favorites and it just started. Now stay on this sofa and watch it or game shows or whatever, but promise me you'll rest for a while."

"I promise."

He nodded. "Good. I'll be back to check on you later."

"That's not—"

"Don't argue with me, Erin."

She pursed her lips, but then nodded.

"I'll see myself out. Take it easy."

Erin watched him go through half-lidded eyes. With a sigh, she stretched out on the sofa while resting her head on a pillow. She was almost asleep when the scene unfolding on the television captured her attention. A beautiful blonde in a silky red teddy and a raven-haired, shirtless, hard-bodied man were kissing passionately while in bed.

Erin blinked, trying to stay focused. The man nibbled on her neck while running his hand up her bare thigh. The woman sighed dramatically and then begged the man to make love to her. He responded by kissing her deeply. . . .

Erin drifted off while listening to whispered words of love, long-lasting sighs. By the time the program cut to a toilet paper commercial, she was fast asleep. . . .

And dreaming . . .

His thumbs hooked into the thin straps of her red teddy and, with one gentle tug, brought the lacy silk to her waist. His green eyes darkened with desire as he bent his head slowly toward her breasts and took one hardened nipple into his hot mouth while palm-

ing the other in his hand. Erin moaned softly at the sweet sensation uncurling in her stomach, and wanted the moment to last forever.

"Michael," she murmured as the pleasure began to build.

∽ chapter
eight

As he drove down Maple Street, Michael tried to shake the worry nagging at his brain. He had seen heat exhaustion too many times not to take it seriously. Would she rest? Drink plenty of fluids? *I should have stayed with her for a while*, he thought.

Cursing under his breath, he did a U-turn and pulled back into her driveway. He hopped out of the car and sprinted as fast as his leg would allow. He had snagged her key so he could lock the door on his way out and used it to quietly let himself back in.

He breathed a sigh of relief when he saw that she was sleeping on the sofa. Walking softly toward her, he picked up the remote, grinned at the steamy bedroom scene, and then turned the television off.

Erin moaned, drawing a glance of concern from him. He crept closer and knelt down by the sofa.

"Erin?" he whispered. Her eyelids fluttered but remained shut. With the curtains drawn, filtered fingers of sunshine dimly lit the room, but when he leaned closer, Michael could see that her cheeks were flushed.

He placed a hand on her forehead, suddenly afraid that she was running a fever, but she felt only slightly warm. Her breathing, though, was a bit ragged and she moaned again, but he realized . . . it was a moan of *pleasure*.

Hot damn. Little Miss Prim and Proper was having a *wet dream*. He frowned. Did women have those? She let out a breathy sigh. Apparently they did. Feeling like he was intruding on something private, Michael started to push up from his position next to her.

And then she said his name. No, *moaned* his name. Well, hell. The thought that she was having a good time with him and he wasn't on the receiving end didn't seem, well, quite fair.

Michael leaned over her and placed a soft but lingering kiss on her parted lips. He ran his hand up her smooth thigh, stopping his exploration at the edge of her shorts. She quivered in response, and his heart started to thud.

She was oh so hot and ready.

"Erin?" he whispered into her ear, and then pulled back to see her face.

Her eyelids fluttered, but she seemed reluctant to wake up, so he tried again. "Erin, baby. Wake up."

"Michael?" Her voice sounded throaty . . . aroused, and she managed to open her eyes. She blinked, seemed confused.

"I'm right here."

She frowned. "But—"

Michael smothered the rest of her thought with a hot kiss and then joined her on the sofa. She felt warm and pliant beneath him. A soft moan vibrated in the back of her throat as she kissed him back. Her hands slipped underneath his white tank shirt and flattened on his back, palming, then kneading his bare skin.

Michael rocked his hips, rubbing his erection between her legs while kissing her deeply. Arching her back, she rocked with him, driving him crazy with need.

"Erin?" His low growl was a cross between a plea and a demand. He wanted her not only willing but wide-awake. Pushing up on his elbows, he looked down into her flushed face and felt relief when he saw that her green eyes were wide open.

She seemed a bit stunned, but had the flushed look of a woman highly aroused. "I—I was dreaming."

He smiled. "About me?"

She swallowed, turned her face, but nodded.

With gentle fingers, Michael turned her face back so he could look into her eyes. He rocked slightly against her, hot and hard against her pliant softness. "Let me make your dream a reality, Erin."

She blinked up at him but remained silent for a long torturous moment. When she finally opened her mouth to speak, Michael was afraid she would refuse his offer, so he covered her mouth with his, kissing away her qualms. He kissed her with long, coaxing strokes of his tongue until her fists, which clenched his cotton shirt, relaxed.

"Tell me about your dream, Erin. What were we doing?" He nuzzled her neck and nibbled on her ear while moving his hand closer to the pulsing heat between her legs.

"Making love."

"Where?"

"In bed."

In one swift movement Michael stood up, leaned over, and scooped her up into his arms.

"Wh-what are you doing?"

"Making your dreams come true." He strode down the short hallway and easily found her bedroom. He laid her gently against a mound of frilly pillows and then turned to pull the shades down.

"Now, what were you wearing?"

"A red teddy."

Michael glanced at her dresser and then asked hopefully, "Do you have a red teddy?"

"No."

Well, damn. "Okay, what was I wearing?"

"Nothing."

He grinned. "Well, that's easy enough." With one swift tug, he pulled his shirt over his head and tossed it onto the floor. A moment later he stepped out of his shorts and peeled off his briefs.

"Your wish, sleeping beauty, is my command."

chapter nine

Somewhere, way in the back of her mind, Erin knew she should put an end to what was about to happen. Warning bells, however, were drowned out by the hot waves of desire she felt while gazing at Michael's naked body.

He was long and lean, with whipcord strength that could throw a baseball over ninety-five miles per hour. He didn't have those bulky machine-generated muscles, but rather had the hard, honed look of a natural athlete.

"This is your dream, Erin. Just tell me what you want." He came to the edge of the bed and let her look her fill.

Her breath caught in her throat and she pushed up to her knees. With shaking hands, she reached up and trailed her fingertips over the springy, silky hair of his chest and down his abdomen, but then hesitated. He was proudly erect—so big, so thick. She was fascinated and, oh, *so* wanted to hold him, stroke him.

"Touch me, Erin." His voice sounded gruff, strained.

With her heart pounding in her ears, she slowly reached forward and lightly cupped his sac. She watched as he shivered and inhaled with a sharp hiss when she slid her hand up around the base of his penis. He felt hot, steely hard, and pulsing with power. She tightened her grip and slid her hand up the length of him and then back down. With the fingertip of her other hand, she touched the head of his penis where a pearly drop appeared. She swirled the silky hot liquid around the smooth head with the pad of her fingertip.

"God, Erin."

She glanced up at his face. A muscle jumped in his jaw. His penis pulsed and throbbed in her hand. She had never taken a man in her mouth, never thought she would want to, but suddenly . . . she did. She wanted to give him pleasure in the most intimate of acts. She wanted to taste him on her tongue, feel the strength, the heat of him filling her mouth.

Erin was shaking, wild with wanting him. She leaned forward and would have taken him into her mouth, but he pushed gently at her shoulders and stepped back.

"No, God, Erin, I'm ready to burst. One touch of that sweet mouth and I'll explode!"

"But—"

He put a fingertip to her lips. "I want to make love to you, Erin. Come inside you. This is your dream, remember?"

Erin nodded and then frowned when he turned away, stooped down, and fished for something in his pants. He opened his wallet and found a condom. Good Lord, she hadn't even thought of *that*. Safe sex was preached to her students, and here she was about to break every basic rule that she lived by. Reality check, Erin. "Michael."

"Yes?" He turned to her and smiled. Not a wolfish I'm-getting-a-piece-of-ass smile, but a real smile, and she melted.

"Come to me." She held out her arms. He joined her on the bed, pushed her back against the pillows, and kissed her deeply. She wrapped her arms around his neck, holding him close. She had never been kissed this way, with such desire, such passion. Her heart thumped; her body pulsed, tingled. His hand slid up her calf to her thigh, skimmed beneath her shirt, over her quivering belly, and then cupped her breast.

"Take off your clothes," he growled into her ear. "I want you naked."

Erin nodded and lifted her hips so he could tug her shorts and panties off. She sat up and pulled her shirt over her head while he unhooked her bra.

"Let me look at you," he said softly.

Erin should have felt shy beneath his smoldering gaze, but she didn't. She felt beautiful. Desired. She let him look, touch . . .

Taste.

"Oh!" His fingers shimmered lightly down her belly while his mouth captured one tight nipple. He licked in a swirling motion and then nipped sharply with his teeth at the same moment that he inserted one long finger into her slick folds. With a strangled cry, she arched up against his hand, making his finger go deeper. He feasted on one breast and then the other until her breath came in short gasps. Moving in a delicious downward path, he kissed, licked, nuzzled, until his head was between her legs.

"Michael, no!" She protested and tried to lift her head from the pillows, but she felt too weak, too heavy.

"Just one taste," he pleaded, and covered her sex with his hot mouth.

Shocked at the intense pleasure, she arched up, opening wide for his greedy tongue. "Michael!" She wanted him to stop. This was too . . . too *much*. Clutching at the pillows, she gasped when he thrust his tongue deep, parting her with his fingers so she was exposed, open and glistening. He nipped at her clitoris with his teeth, and the blinding pleasure intensified. With one last long lick, he covered her body with his and kissed her deeply, shocking her, *arousing her* with the taste of her own essence.

"Wrap your legs around me. Tell me how you want to be loved. Slow and easy? Or hard and fast?" The tip of his penis touched her throbbing clit, teasing, waiting.

"Slow," she managed to say, and he slipped inside in one smooth move. God, he filled her to the hilt and then he pulled out ever so slowly, again, and then again. The slow strokes were agonizing. "No, no, no! Faster!"

"Like this?" He quickened his pace.

"Yes!" Erin scooted her legs up around his waist and held on to his neck.

"And this?" He went deeper, moved even faster, stealing her breath.

Erin could only hold on with her head thrown back while he filled her completely. He was so big, so strong—such raw power. His muscles bunched and quivered while his back became slick with sweat. Her heart pounded and her entire body tingled with the anticipation of blessed release. Each stroke sent her higher, closer.

"Please." Desperate, she matched him stroke for stroke in a frenzied rhythm that had them panting, until he tensed, grabbed her ass, and entered her deeper than she'd thought possible, sending her flying over the edge with an intense orgasm that had her gasping, gripping his shoulders while she floated outside herself and then tumbled back to earth dazed and shaking.

Dimly, she felt the pulsing power of his release. He groaned and captured her mouth in a searing kiss before rolling over onto his back, taking her with him.

Erin collapsed, placing her cheek on his damp chest. She inhaled the spice of his cologne, the heady musk of sex and sweat. They were still intimately connected and he seemed to want to keep it that way. When she tried to pull away, he cupped her bottom and began to move his hips in a slow easy rhythm that had her rocking gently with him.

Erin pushed up, splayed her hands against his chest, and continued to move while his big hands on her ass lifted, guided, causing a slow burn. She caught her bottom lip between her teeth. He was so big and her flesh so tender, swollen. It was, oh, God . . . sweet *agony*. Pain and then building of such pleasure. Moving, moaning, she watched his face through half-lidded eyes. His heart thudded beneath her palms. His breathing quickened, but he kept the pace slow and easy . . . slow and . . .

"Michael." His name was torn from her throat as she climaxed again, bringing him right along with her. Corded muscles strained as he arched up, thrust deep, while holding her close.

No words of love were exchanged, but Erin was blown away by the intensity of the moment. For her, this was more than mind-numbing sex. Michael Manning had just touched something deep within her heart, her soul.

"Oh, damn you, Michael Manning!" she muttered darkly.

"What?"

"Damn you, damn you . . . *damn you!*"

∽ chapter
ten

"Ouch!" Michael rubbed where she smacked him on the chest. He grabbed for her as she rolled off of him and tumbled to the floor.

"You okay?" He sat up and peered over the side of the bed and was met with an if-looks-could-kill glare. He frowned down at her. "What in the hell did I do?"

"You ruined me, you . . . you *son of a bitch*."

His lips twitched. "Do you know you cuss like a sailor when you're agitated?" But then he frowned. "Ruined you? You mean your reputation? Erin, I won't tell—"

"That's not what I mean!" She stood up and stomped her foot, causing her awesome breasts to jiggle. Her nipples were rosy from his mouth. God, she was beautiful—no, make that *crazy*.

"Hey, stop that!" A pillow hit him in the head and

bounced to the floor. "Erin, what in the hell is wrong with you? What do you mean I've ruined you?"

"For . . . for sex!" She blushed hotly and turned away.

Ooh, so Miss Prim and Proper's potty mouth was popping off again. Michael frowned, but then had to grin. "I think that's an oxymoron or something." Oh, shit, her eyes were filling with tears. Shit, shit, shit. "Erin, what's wrong?"

"I knew it would be like this with you." Her voice was husky, thick with unshed tears.

Michael swung his legs over the side of the bed and angled his head at her. "Erin—"

"And now nobody else can measure up."

Michael's eyebrows lifted and he blinked at her. "Thank you . . . I think."

She glared over her shoulder at him, putting him at a complete loss. He didn't want this to end like this, damn it. "You weren't half bad yourself." His attempt at humor was met with the thinning of her lips, and then she bent over to pick up her panties, giving a view that had him getting hard all over again.

"Erin," he began in what he thought was a reasonable tone of voice, but got pissed when she threw his shorts at his face. He headed for the bathroom to flush the condom and hurried back to face her. "What in the hell is going on here?" Michael prided himself on knowing the wiles of women, but she was throwing him a curveball. He never could hit a damn curve.

He watched her yank her shirt over her head. She was a bundle of emotion, and he didn't know if he should comfort her or yell at her, but he sure as hell wasn't going to let her toss him out on his ear.

"You can go now." With a lift of her chin, she pointed to the door, dismissing him like he was one of her students.

"I'm not going anywhere until you tell me what's going on in that red head of yours." He stood up, crossed his arms over his chest, but remained brazenly naked.

She planted her hands on her hips and angled her head to look up at him. "You got what you wanted, Michael. I'm sure you usually do." She waved her hand in the direction of the rumpled bed. "This might be a common occurrence for you, but—"

"Ah, so you've got me all figured out, do you?" he interrupted with a sigh, and then began putting on his clothes. "And here I thought you were different." He couldn't quite keep the sadness out of his voice, and that finally gave her pause.

"What do you mean?" The schoolmarm tone remained, but she sounded a little less sure of herself.

"I grew up in this small town, the son of a preacher. I might have rebelled against my daddy, but some of his fire and brimstone rubbed off on me. I'm not nearly as big of a bad boy as you might believe, Miss O'Shea." Michael tugged his tank over his head and then gave her a shake of his head. "God knows I'm not perfect, but I do have standards."

She took a step toward him. "Michael—"

He held up a hand. "Don't bother," he warned, and then chuckled harshly. "I'm sorry that I pissed you off by being such a good lover, but I'll let you in on a little secret." He leaned forward, ignoring the slight tremble of her bottom lip. "What just happened in that bed was incredible, but it wasn't because I was some hotshot washed-up ball player that has fucked a thousand women."

"Michael, stop! I didn't mean—"

"Yes, you did. You thought you had me pegged." He shrugged his shoulders. "Part of it was my own fault for being such a smart-ass to begin with, and part of it was your fault for giving me a dumb-jock stereotype." He shrugged again. "I can deal with the stereotype. I've had to all my life. But not your holier-than-thou attitude. And not your pity. That, I can't handle. Never could." He pointed to the bed. "What happened here today, Miss O'Shea, was a joint decision, but if you want to blame me, well, then, suit yourself."

She looked up at him, her eyes swimming with unshed tears. "I don't blame you for this. I blame myself."

He laughed again without humor. "Blame? Why don't you just come right out and say *regret*? Do you regret what just happened, Erin?" He looked at her, his heart pounding while he waited for an answer. Why did this hurt so much?

A tear rolled down her cheek, giving him his answer. He reached over and brushed the teardrop away with the pad of his thumb. "I'm sorry that you feel such guilt and regret for what we just shared." God, he sounded like a fucking *girl*. He drew in a long shaky breath and then let it out. "But before I leave, let me tell you one more thing."

"Michael, don't do this."

He shook his head and then chuckled darkly. "Since you've cut my nuts off, I might as well hand them to you on a platter."

She put a hand on his chest and looked up at him with big beseeching eyes. "Michael, you've got this all wrong. Listen to me—"

He put a silencing finger to her lips. "I'll make this easy for you. You regret sleeping with me. I regret this too, but for very different reasons."

"And just what are your reasons?" Her voice was low and heavy with emotion.

Michael shook his head. He suddenly didn't want to let her in on the fact that she had touched him on a level much deeper than sensational sex.

"You see, I'm the one who has you pegged." He gave her a sad smile. "You remind me of my sister Rachel. All prim and proper on the outside. Too good for a big and bad male. She finally came to her senses before it was too late. Maybe someday you will too."

Erin watched him walk out the door and leave the house, and didn't know what to do or say to make him stay. She felt wretched because much of what he said was true. She *had* judged him. Thought him shallow, put him in a category he didn't deserve to be in. The question now was how to make it up to him.

Erin watched Michael roar away in his sleek, fast car. She shook her head as two things became painfully clear. One, she had somehow managed to hurt tough-guy Michael Manning on two separate occasions. Two, she was head over heels in love with the man and on some level always had been. Now the question remained. What in the world was she going to do about it?

"I need a game plan," Erin mumbled under her breath. "And I need it quick."

chapter eleven

A game plan was hard as hell to put into action when the other player chose to avoid you altogether. Erin found all kinds of reasons to be at school during the following week while the baseball camp was going on. As Michael had promised, naming him as the new coach had the camp full of participants with a long waiting list. She watched from her office window while Michael showed the fundamentals of pitching to the large group of eight- to fourteen-year-olds. He wore a brace on his leg, but she was relieved to see that his leg seemed to be holding up.

Erin grinned when he gave a high five to a towheaded youngster who finally got the ball over the plate. He had a way with the kids, and he let the varsity players who were helping out at the camp joke around with him, but he demanded respect as well.

Erin knew that the state championship he promised wasn't out of the question.

As if feeling her gaze upon him, he suddenly glanced up at her window, but before she could raise her hand to wave, he turned away.

"Erin?"

She jumped at the sound of her name. "Oh, Dan. Hi!" She turned to face him. "Camp is going well, isn't it?"

Dan nodded as he hitched up his shorts, which were riding low on his belly. "Michael has a way with them boys. Once they got over the fact that Michael Manning was their coach, they got down to the business of baseball."

"You were right about him, Dan. Now, what can I do for you?"

"Well, some of the kids begged Michael to get some of the old tapes from when he played here in high school. I need the keys to the storage room off the library to round the tapes up. We're going to let the kids watch them in the gym in the air-conditioning to get them out of the damn heat." He mopped his sweaty brow with a handkerchief.

"Oh, sure." Erin frowned. "You look overheated, Dan. You go on down to the gym and I'll bring the tapes down to you."

He nodded. "I am feeling a bit woozy."

"Go get a cold drink." Erin shook her head, making her ponytail swing back and forth. "This August heat has been brutal. I was about to head home, but I'll get the tapes first."

Erin headed down the hall, opened the library door,

and headed over to the storage room. After unlocking the door, she stepped inside the large dark room crammed full of shelves. The sports memorabilia were all the way toward the back in a separate room. She sneezed from the dust motes swirling in the stuffy room and felt her way around for the light switch.

"Dan? Make sure you get the tapes from my eighth-grade year as well. I want to show—" Michael began, and then sneezed. "Where the hell is the light switch?"

"Bless you," Erin offered, and was met with silence in the dark room. For a moment she thought Michael had left, but then he answered, or rather *growled*.

"Where is Dan?"

"Cooling off—ouch!" She had bumped into something with her shin. "Where *is* the light switch, anyway?"

"Try over by the far wall." His deep voice was close to her ear, making her acutely aware of his presence in the dark room. His arm brushed up against her shoulder as he reached past her, groping for the switch.

"There," he said. "I found it." Flickering florescent light flooded the room.

"Oh, my God, it's a mouse!" Erin squealed and backed up just as the little critter scurried underneath a box directly in front of her. She came up against the hard wall of Michael's chest and yelped when another rodent ran past her. She turned and grabbed a handful of his damp T-shirt.

"Erin, it's only a mouse," he said dryly.

"Mice," she corrected, her heart pounding in fear. She spotted a gray tail and twisted her fist into his shirt. "Oh, my God, they are *everywhere*. Get me out of here!" She tried to push past him, but he snagged her around the waist. "Let me go!" She struggled, but he held her firmly against his body.

"No! I need to get the damned tapes. Now, point them out and then you can get the hell out of here."

Erin swallowed and then took a cleansing breath. "It's only mice, it's only mice," she chanted as she pointed to the opposite wall. "The top shelf, I think," she said, trying to regain her dignity and almost succeeding when a little bitty mouse ran across the floor just a few feet in front of her. She bit her bottom lip to keep from screaming, but flattened her back against him.

Michael frowned when he felt her tremble and realized that she was really scared. Still holding her around the waist, he leaned his mouth close to her ear. "Erin, calm down," he said in what he hoped was a soothing voice. Difficult when having her sweet little body plastered against him while his arm nestled just beneath her breasts.

She nodded, but he could feel the wild pounding of her heart. "Wh—when I was a kid, th-there was a mouse in my sleeping bag. I—felt it, but—the zipper got stuck and it crawled all over me, trying to get away from my thrashing legs." She shivered. "I've been petrified ever since. Silly, I know . . . oh, God, there is another one!"

"Erin, it's the same one. I won't let them get near you. They are more scared of you than you are of them." He felt her heart continue to pound and her breath come in short gasps.

"I don't think so. Michael, please get me out of here."

He loosened his hold on her waist. "Okay. You go on. I'll find the tapes."

She nodded and took a wobbly step toward the door.

"Whoa, hey, let me help." He hooked his arm around her waist, lifted her up, and carried her out of the room.

"This is becoming a habit of yours," she tried to joke.

"Can you stand?"

"I—I think so. God, I feel so stupid." She lifted her head from his shoulder and looked at him. "I'm sorry for being such a weenie." Her chin came up. "I'm usually pretty brave about stuff."

"Is that so?" Michael cocked an eyebrow and tried not to grin. He was completely forgetting how pissed off he was at her. Keeping his distance had been harder than hell, and holding her in his arms was *making* him harder than hell. Continual thoughts of her 24-7 had him losing sleep, and more than once, he had picked up the phone to call her. Had even driven by her house, for pity's sake.

And now he had her in his arms. His gaze lowered to her mouth, just inches from his. She licked her lips and he had to kiss her or die. And then some fucking buzzer went off, startling them both, and brought him back to his senses. "What the hell was that?"

"Lunch bell. Sorry."

He put her down, hoping that the bulge in his shorts wasn't too evident. "You can go now. I can get the tapes." He turned back toward the storage room, needing to put some distance between them.

"Michael?"

He paused and looked over his shoulder, trying to give her the impression of disinterest. "Yeah?"

She looked at him for a long moment, making his heart pound in anticipation, and then finally spoke. "You're doing a great job with those kids. I can tell you're going to be an awesome coach."

Nothing she could have said would have pleased him more. This past week had given his life purpose, meaning. For the first time in a long while, he was looking forward to getting up in the morning. He carefully schooled his features, and hoping to keep the emotion out of his voice, he replied, "Thank you."

She nodded, looked like she wanted to say more. He turned away, but could feel her eyes following him. Michael had felt her gaze on him all week and told himself she was just watching to see how he was doing. He reminded himself how much she loved baseball and tried to convince himself she was looking out for the school, the kids.

But he knew better. There was something between them that could not be denied no matter how pissed off he was at her.

Michael blew out a long sigh while reaching for the tapes. Damn her! He didn't need this kind of complication when things were finally falling into place. With a grunt, he pulled the box down from the shelf and vowed to keep Erin off of his mind . . . and out of his bed.

Michael limped down the hallway, lugging the

heavy box of tapes. He knew watching them was going to be hard. The kids were on lunch break, giving him time to view a little of the state championship game in private. Hopefully he would have his composure before the kids filed into the locker room to watch him pitch the best game of his high school career.

Michael slipped the tape into the VCR and straddled a chair. He grinned when he saw a younger, forty-pounds-thinner Dan giving the team a pep talk just before the game began. A funny feeling hit him in the gut when he watched a younger version of himself walk out to the pitcher's mound. This was when he had dreams of making the majors. When the future looked bright and promising.

Michael absently rubbed his leg while forcing himself to watch the game that had solidified a college scholarship and paved his way to major-league baseball.

"You pitched a great game, Michael."

"Dan, I didn't know you were in here."

He shrugged. "I was feeling a little overheated. Erin suggested that I come in here and cool off."

Michael turned his attention to the television screen. "I struggled that first inning."

"You were all keyed up, and that damned umpire behind the plate wasn't giving you much of a strike zone."

Michael watched as he walked the first batter, removed his ball cap, and wiped the sweat from his dripping brow. He pitched another curve that looked like it caught the corner of the plate.

"That was a damned strike," Dan grumbled.

The hometown crowd agreed, with some boos directed at the ump. The next pitch was a fastball right down the plate, followed by a curve that looked pretty good as well, but the umpire signaled a ball.

The crowd collectively groaned, but one high-pitched yell could be heard clearly above the rest. The camera zoomed in on a skinny redhead with her hands cupped to her mouth. "When was the last time you had your eyes checked? That was a strike!"

Dan chuckled. "That Erin looks so innocent, but she sure can be a little spitfire."

Michael snorted. "Tell me something I *don't* know."

"She's sweet on you."

Michael turned to Dan with a straight face but a thumping heart. "Now, why do you say that?"

Dan shrugged and his face turned a little ruddy. "It's in the way she looks at you." He nodded toward the television. "She always did have a crush on you. Was always asking me about you after you left."

Michael shrugged. "She likes baseball."

"She likes you."

"Dan, she made it pretty clear how low her opinion is of me. Your uptight little principal thinks I'm nothing more than a dumb jock."

"Yeah, right." Dan rolled his eyes. "That's nothing more than a defense mechanism."

Michael raised his eyebrows. "Explain that statement to a dumb jock."

Dan rewound the tape and freeze-framed Erin with her hands cupped over her mouth. "Homely teenage girl has a huge crush on hotshot ballplayer. Homely teenage girl blossoms into a beautiful woman, and hotshot ballplayer comes back to town."

Michael grinned. "And she can't get it through her red head that hotshot ballplayer is falling in love with her."

Dan grinned back at him. "See, you're not really just a dumb jock after all."

Michael shook his head. "Now what am I going to do about the mess I've created? I let my hotshot pride push her away."

Dan poked a finger in his chest. "What you need, hotshot, is a game plan."

Michael angled his head at Dan. "And you think you can come up with a strategy?"

Dan pointed to the television. "How do you think we won that state championship?"

Michael jammed a thumb at his chest. "You had me."

"Exactly."

Michael laughed. He could see the wheels turning in his old coach's head.

Dan removed his ball cap and scratched his head. "We need a reason to get Erin over to your place. Got any thoughts?"

Michael frowned for a minute and then snapped his fingers. "I've got to babysit my five-month-old niece tonight for my sister, Rachel."

"You . . . babysit an infant?"

"Hey, Brooke likes her Uncle Michael. I happen to be very good with her."

Dan rubbed his hands together. "This is perfect.

Just perfect. Chicks dig men with babies. Now, this is what we do. . . ."

Michael smiled as he listened to Dan's plan, which was just crazy enough to work. Dan had always understood him and had in many ways been more like a father to him than his own. Dan had accepted his faults, encouraged his dreams, and been there for him when his world had been falling apart.

"You like her, don't you, Dan?" he asked softly, already knowing the answer.

"She's the best. If I was thirty years younger, I'd give you a run for your money." He gave Michael a shove. "Now go get the girl."

chapter
twelve

Erin closed the drawer to her file cabinet. Her office was spotless, organized, and ready for the beginning of the new school year. She couldn't come up with one more reason to hang around the school. She sighed. Besides, Michael had made it quite clear that he wanted to keep his distance. She had screwed things up with him, and her game plan had fallen flat on its face.

She picked up the remote to the television, which had been keeping her company while she worked, and was about to turn it off when a news story about the new minor-league baseball stadium being built in her town caught her attention. Chase Mitchell—former major-league superstar shortstop and the newly hired manager of the Sander's City Flyers—and the city mayor were posing with shovels for a classic groundbreaking ceremony.

"Woowee. Now there's a reason to get season tickets. That man is mighty fine."

Erin turned and her mouth dropped open in surprise. Her drama and speech teacher, Josey Cooper, stood with her hands on her hips staring up at the television. At least she thought it was Josey. The slight Southern accent was the same, but that was about it. Josey caught her staring and giggled. Embarrassed, Erin snapped her sagging jaw shut. "You . . . you—"

"Had some work done." Josey did a little spin with her hands in the air. "I put some of my divorce settlement to good use. A little tuck, a little lift, and a personal trainer." She shrugged her tan shoulders and fluffed her sassy new cut highlighted with streaks of blond. "What do you think?" She pursed her pink glossy lips and waited.

"I think you look great," Erin said with a smile. The forty-year-old teacher could easily have passed for thirty, but it wasn't the physical change that had Erin smiling; it was the new attitude she was sporting. She radiated strength and determination, something the bubbly teacher had lost during her painful divorce last year. Erin angled her head at Josey. "You look better than great. You look sassy."

"Ooh, sassy. I like it." She grinned and then winked. "You know what they say. Looking good is the best revenge."

Erin's smile faltered a bit. Revenge? That sounded like she wasn't over her ex, whom she had caught cheating. "Are you doing okay, Josey?" Erin asked softly. She was more than just one of her teachers. She was a friend.

Josey nodded. "I'm ready to get on with my life." She pointed to the television, where the newscaster was announcing that season tickets were going on sale that afternoon. "As a matter of fact, I'd like to get some action like Susan Sarandon and Kevin Costner in *Bull Durham*. Whadaya say, Erin? You love baseball. Let's go get some tickets right smack behind the home-team dugout, girlfriend."

Erin grinned. "I had planned on getting season tickets, but you're kidding about the *Bull Durham* part, right?"

Josey wiggled her eyebrow up and down. "Oh, by the way," she said as she nudged Erin with her elbow, "great job snagging Michael Manning as our new varsity baseball coach. I smell state championship."

Erin nodded. "He'll make a good coach."

Josey smiled and shook her head, making her wispy new haircut flutter around her face. "I was a student teacher the year he streaked across the baseball field. I wonder if he is still as wild as he was in high school. He sure was a hottie." She cocked an eyebrow. "Maybe I'll go to the high school games as well."

Erin got a weird feeling in her stomach and swallowed. The thought of Michael with someone else made her feel . . . oh, God . . . *jealous*. "I could introduce you," she offered, a bit stiffly.

"Oh, my god. Erin, you've got the hots for him. Is he single?"

"Yes, he is single and *no*, I don't have the hots for him!"

"You lie."

Erin opened her mouth to protest, but the sound of

masculine laughter shut them both up. Josey peeped her blond-streaked head out of the office door and then turned to Erin with her hand to her perky new chest.

"Oh, my God, it's Michael Manning and he's talking to none other than Chase Mitchell." She grabbed Erin's arm. "Call them in here and introduce me. Good Lord, Chase is even more handsome in person!"

"No!"

Josey rolled her eyes and then marched over to the doorway. Erin noticed that she had a new sway to her walk and a proud lift of her head. A new attitude, she thought, could be a very good thing.

Josey poked her head out the office door. "Oh, Mr. Manning? Miss O'Shea wants to see you in her office." She turned back around and mouthed, "Here they come!"

Michael entered the office a moment later with Chase Mitchell at his side. Josey was right. Chase was a knockout in person. Retired from pro baseball, he was, Erin guessed, around forty or so. Not handsome in the classic sense, he nonetheless oozed masculinity in a rough, Harrison Ford kind of way. She glanced at his left hand and noticed the absence of a wedding ring.

"You wanted to see me, Miss O'Shea?" Michael felt a stab of jealousy at the way Erin was sizing up Chase, which made his voice sound a little harsh.

"Oh, um, yes."

Michael ground his teeth together and waited impatiently.

Chase nudged him. "Aren't you going to introduce me?"

"Allow me to introduce myself," Josey cut in, and offered her hand to Chase. "I'm Josey Cooper, drama and speech teacher here at Sander's High. We're so glad to have you as manager of the Sander's City Flyers. Erin and I are buying our season tickets this very afternoon. I regret that we have to wait until next spring for the season to begin, Mr. Mitchell."

"Why, thank you for the warm welcome, Ms. Cooper."

"Do call me Josey."

He angled his head at her. "Only if you call me Chase."

Michael wanted to roll his eyes, but refrained. He and Chase had played one season together before his accident. He had forgotten how much of a player Chase was, and the hot little drama teacher was buying his crap big-time. "Chase, this is Erin O'Shea, the school principal."

"Nice to meet you, Erin," Chase said, ticking Michael off when he held on to her hand a moment too long.

"Chase has been kind enough to give a talk to our baseball campers." Michael looked at his watch. "In fact they should be finished watching the tapes. We should get going."

Chase nodded and released Erin's hand. He tipped his Sander's City Flyers ball cap. "Nice to meet you ladies."

"Same here," Josey cooed, and Michael had to all but drag Chase out of the office.

"Hey, I was just about to ask them to join us for dinner later on."

"I've got to babysit my sister's kid."

Chase adjusted his ball cap. "You babysit? You gotta be shittin' me."

"I shit you not, and I'm quite good with her."

Chase chuckled and slapped him on the back. "You always did have women drooling all over you. Now, if I were you, I'd go after that hot little redhead."

"I'm one step ahead of ya, bro."

chapter
thirteen

Michael sat Brooke down in her bouncy seat and picked up the phone. He dialed Erin's number and tried not to feel guilty about the line of bull he was going to tell her. When she answered the phone with that throaty voice of hers, he started weaving his tale.

"Erin, I need your help."

"Michael, what's wrong?"

"My sister dropped her baby off for me to watch, and I'm at a loss. Geez, Erin, she's so tiny, I'm afraid to even pick her up. She's sleeping now, but when she wakes up I'll be in a panic. Can you come over and help me? I wouldn't ask, but I'm desperate."

"Okay, I'll be right over."

Michael hung up the phone and grinned down at Brooke, who gurgled up at him. "Work with me, Brooke. We gotta make this look good."

Michael mussed up his hair, untucked his oxford

shirt from his jean shorts, and tried to look frazzled. He picked up Brooke and looked out the front window for Erin's Mustang to arrive. Brooke teethed on her fist and watched with him, totally content to be in his arms.

"Okay, here she comes, Brooke. Give Uncle Michael a pout." He stuck his bottom lip out. Brooke giggled and grabbed at his protruding lip, smacking her wet hand on his face. Michael sighed and kissed the tip of her nose. When the doorbell rang, he waited a moment and then answered it.

"Oh, thank God," he said with a huge sigh. "Come on in."

"Oh, my, she's beautiful, Michael. What is her name?"

"Brooke."

"Oh, how pretty," she cooed at the baby, but then turned a questioning gaze to him. "She sure looks content. What is the problem?"

"Well . . . ah, none . . . *now* but you should have seen her thirty minutes ago. Whew, I didn't think I'd ever get her calmed down." As if she understood that he was handing Erin a line, Brooke fisted her tiny hand into his chest hair and tugged . . . hard. "Ouch!" Brooke giggled and Erin joined in. "Women," he grumbled. "You're all in this together."

Brooke stuck out her bottom lip and her little chin quivered.

"I didn't mean it. Oh, God, sweetie, please don't cry." He unbuttoned his shirt. "Here, tug all you want."

If Erin *thought* she was in love with Michael, she

knew it now. And what was it about seeing a grown man holding a baby that was so incredibly sexy?

The doorbell rang and Erin held out her arms. "Here, I'll take her." Michael placed Brooke in her arms and her breath caught. Oh, she loved babies. The powdery smell, the soft skin.

Michael opened the door. "Rachel. You're back early."

Erin frowned. For someone who was so desperate, he sounded a bit disappointed to be relieved of his babysitting duties.

"I know. A business call for Jake cut our dinner short. How was she? Good for you as usual?"

Michael looked at Erin and gave her a sheepish grin. "Busted," he said, and her insides turned to mush.

Brooke reached her chubby arms for her mother, and Erin handed her over.

"You must be Erin. I'm Rachel, Michael's sister."

Erin held out her hand. "It's nice to meet you. Brooke is beautiful."

"Thank you." She turned to Michael. "Hey, I would appreciate it if you would take a ride down to the cabin this weekend. Jake and I haven't gotten a chance to get there in a while and I want to make sure everything is okay."

Michael nodded, understanding her offer, and grinned. "I could do that."

Rachel leaned over and kissed him. "Great. Listen, I've got to run. Nice to met you, Erin." She hefted her diaper bag over her shoulder and headed out the door with Brooke.

Michael closed the door and turned to Erin.

"She sure left in a hurry."

"She knew I wanted to be alone with you."

Erin took a step closer to him. "This was a setup, wasn't it?"

"Yeah. Dan told me chicks dig men with babies."

"Dan was right." She closed the gap between them and splayed her hand on his warm chest, exposed by his unbuttoned shirt. She pushed him up against the wall and molded her body to his. "I have never, *ever* wanted a man more than I do at this very moment." She boldly ran her hand over his erection but then turned away.

"Hey," he said hoarsely. "Get back here."

"No." She sashayed away from him. "You drove me crazy with your cold-shoulder treatment all week. I'm going to make you work for it. You're not the only one who can play hardball, Michael Manning."

Michael was on her in three long strides. He picked her up and tossed her over his shoulder, ignoring her shriek of protest.

"Hey, what are you doing?" She pounded on his back, but he only laughed.

"I'm working for it." He entered his bedroom and bounced her down on his big bed. "In fact, I'm going to have you begging for it." Without taking his eyes from her face, he shrugged out of his shirt, unzipped his pants, and peeled off his underwear.

Erin swallowed. The man was gorgeous. The man was hard. And he was all hers.

Erin pushed up to her knees on the soft surface of the bed. With shaking fingers she tugged her T-shirt over her head and tossed it onto the floor. She stood up, placed her hands on his smooth shoulders where he stood at the edge of the mattress. "Keep working, Michael," she whispered.

"My pleasure," he growled. With a flick of his wrist, he unhooked the front clasp of her bra, making her breasts tumble free. He worked magic with his hands, lovingly cupping her breasts while looking his fill. The heat of his hungry gaze made her heart thump and her body tingle with anticipation of what he would do next.

His nostrils flared, his green eyes gleamed, and then he slowly leaned forward and took one beaded nipple into his hot mouth. A sharp stab of longing had her back arching and her fingers digging into his shoulders. His teasing tongue licked lightly, making her want more.

"Michael . . . *please.*"

"Please, what? Tell me what you want."

Unable to speak, she let his head droop to the side and threaded her fingers through his hair, pushing her breast into his mouth. Her body language was all he needed. He feasted on her breasts, first one and then the other, leaving her nipples shiny and wet.

"Is that what you wanted?" he finally asked.

She nodded while he worked the button and zipper of her shorts. He tugged them down over her hips while she clung to his shoulders. His erection, smooth, hard, and oh so hot, brushed against her thigh. Her legs trembled and she would have tumbled to the bed, but he cupped her ass with firm, steadying hands.

She stood before him clad only in peach-colored silk panties. "Take them off of me," she whispered.

"Not just yet." Instead, he inched her closer to his face and then dipped his head to nuzzle her mound, wetting the silk, teasing her clitoris with his tongue. Nibbling against the wet barrier, he refused to remove her panties, making her wild with the need to have him against her naked skin.

"Michael, take—"

"No!" He nuzzled, nibbled, licked at the silk.

"I need—"

"What?"

"Your . . . mmmmouth!"

"Like this?"

Before she could answer, he hooked his thumbs in the sides of her panties and slid them over her hips and swiftly down her legs. With his mouth against her wet, hot sex, he guided her with his hands splayed on her ass to the edge of the mattress as he knelt down on the floor in front of her. Spreading her thighs wider apart, he made sweet love to her with his mouth, licking lightly, making her crave more. When she whimpered, he took pity and applied pressure, flicking his tongue over her clitoris until she was ready to explode.

And then he stopped.

"What?" Her voice was raspy . . . pleading. She tried to raise her head, but her limbs were like lead, and her head was like a bowling ball. She was on fire, throbbing with the need for release. And then she felt him blowing on her, making her shiver, arch up off of the bed in shock. "Michaellll?"

Suddenly his tongue was inside her, pointed, rigid, and thrusting once, twice, and then he licked her hard before sucking on her clitoris. Clutching blindly at his shoulders, his head, Erin came with a white-hot shuddering climax, intense and beautiful.

For a stunned moment, she simply lay there, breathing hard and feeling tingling aftershocks of pleasure while unable to move. Finally, she was able to lift her head and give him a wobbly smile. "Thank you," she said primly, realized how ridiculous she sounded, and laughed.

"My pleasure," he said with a wicked grin. When he turned away, she came up onto her elbows and protested. "What are you doing?" she asked, and then realized he was rolling on a condom. "Oh," she said weakly.

He knelt down on the bed. Erin stared up at him, enjoying the sight of his naked body bathed in the warm glow of the setting sun filtering through the drapes. He straddled her, his muscled thighs poised to make love to her. She reached and cupped his maleness. He shuddered when she ran her hand up the steely hard strength of his penis.

"Kiss me, Michael."

He leaned down on his forearms and captured her mouth in a way that had her arching her body up to make contact with his. The shock of tasting her essence on his lips was erotic, intimate, and wildly arousing. Her breasts grazed his chest and he groaned.

And then he thrust inside her with one smooth

stroke. Slick and ready, still tingling, her body welcomed him, and she moved her hips in a slow, steady, rocking rhythm.

But it wasn't nearly enough. Pleasure began to build and she needed more. Her heart pounded; her breathing quickened.

"Wrap your legs around me, Erin."

She did, allowing him to thrust deeper, harder . . . faster. She went wild with needing him, matching his frenzied pace, which was turning her world into a kaleidoscope of bright colors, moving, shifting . . . and then exploding.

"Michael!" It was a throaty cry of passion, of possession.

Of love.

He grabbed her hips and thrust deep, holding her steady as he climaxed. Erin felt him shudder, loving the sound of intense pleasure from deep in his throat. She opened her eyes and marveled at the beauty of his corded muscles shiny with a thin sheen of sweat. She moved her hands over his shoulders and down his back and cupped his ass.

He chuckled weakly. "Wow." He leaned his forehead against hers and tried to hold his weight off of her but his arms were too shaky. Reluctantly breaking the intimate connection, he rolled to his side and gave her a lazy, contented smile.

Erin rested her cheek on his chest and placed her hand over his wildly beating heart. She drew circles in his silky chest hair while they both attempted to recover. Finally, she was able to lift her head and place a soft kiss on his mouth.

"I'm sorry I misjudged you, Michael."

He reached up and brushed damp tendrils of hair away from her face. "You weren't entirely wrong in your assessment of me."

She frowned. "Yes, I was."

He rubbed his index finger over her swollen bottom lip and shook his head. "I had no intention of taking the coaching job at Sander's High. I thought I was above coaching high school baseball." He grinned and tweaked her nose. "But your snotty attitude ticked me off."

She giggled. "You managed to take *me* down a peg or two."

His grin faded. "When I found out I couldn't pitch anymore, I thought my life was over, not worth living. Baseball was my life."

"That's understandable, Michael."

"Yeah, but wrong. Oddly enough, it was the birth of Brooke that shook me up. I held her in my arms, saw the look of love on Rachel's and Jake's faces, and I knew my life was missing the most important thing of all. I knew then what I wanted out of life—I just didn't think I could ever find it."

Erin felt her throat clog with tears. "Have you found it, Michael?"

"Without a doubt." He kissed her soundly and then cupped her breast, nuzzled her neck, all the while moving his hand increasingly lower until he had her squirming and breathless.

"Michael?"

"Hmmm?" He nibbled on her earlobe.

"I still expect a state championship, you know."

"Then you shall have it. Any other demands?"

"Make love to me all night long."

His laughter rumbled in her ear, sending a delicious shiver down her spine. "Now, that's a job I think I can handle."

heat
wave

∽ chapter
one

Josey Cooper leaned over and handed her friend Erin Manning the flimsy box containing two soft pretzels and two Cokes. "What did I miss?" she asked as she sat down in her stadium seat directly behind the home-team dugout.

Erin brushed the thick coating of coarse salt off of her pretzel. "Nothing much. A fly ball to center moved the runner over, but nobody scored."

Josey nodded and then took a sip of her soft drink. "Good." She grinned as she watched Erin polish off half of her pretzel in record time.

"Hey, don't give me that look. I'm eating for two, you know."

"Don't talk with your mouth full."

Erin grinned. "Impossible, since my mouth is always full."

Josey laughed, but their attention was captured by the loud crack of a bat smacking a baseball. Standing

97

up, she shaded her eyes to the outfield. "Damn, it's a home run!"

Erin groaned. "Chase is going to have to bring in a new pitcher."

Josey nodded her agreement as she plopped back down into her seat. The four-run lead the Sander's City Flyers had was suddenly cut in half. She watched Chase Mitchell, the team manager for the minor-league Flyers, stroll slowly out to the mound. Damn, but that man looked good in a pair of skintight baseball pants.

Erin nudged Josey with her elbow. "Michael invited Chase over for a barbecue on Sunday. You should come."

"I don't know." Josey avoided her best friend's gaze. "Cal is back in town. He invited me to dinner tonight."

"Oh, please. Your divorce has been final for almost a year. Don't get tangled up with that jerk again."

Josey took a long swallow of her cold drink and crunched some ice before answering. "It's only dinner. I'm not going to sleep with the man." She pushed her sunglasses up and watched Chase Mitchell as he signaled for a pitcher from the bull pen.

"Why have dinner with him?"

Josey shrugged her shoulders and turned to face Erin. "I guess I just want to know how things are going with him since he got cut from the soap opera. He sounded so down when he called."

"Cal always comes crawling back when his career takes a nosedive. All the man ever cared about was his doggone acting career." Erin put her hand over her mouth. "Oh, Josey, I'm sorry. I'm sure he cared about you. I didn't mean to be so harsh. It's just that you're starting to get your groove back and he shows up to screw with your head."

Josey patted Erin on the arm. "Maybe I just want to let him see what he gave up."

Erin leaned close and whispered, "*Don't* get sucked in by his charm and his flashy white soap opera smile."

"I won't. I promise! I just want to see how he's doing . . . and, well, maybe make him drool a little." She held up her finger and thumb an inch apart.

"Josey—"

She patted Erin's arm again. "Don't worry. I am *so* over him."

Josey looked into the full-length mirror in her bedroom and gazed at her reflection with a critical eye. The little black dress skimmed her figure and flared out playfully a few inches above the knee. Both tasteful and ultrasexy, the dress was perfect. High-heeled, strappy sandals, a single strand of pearls, and a tiny beaded purse gave her an eat-your-heart-out look.

She headed back into the bathroom for a last-minute makeup check. After adding a bit more peach-tinted lip gloss, she fluffed her chin-length light brown hair recently highlighted with strands of honey blond. Her skin had an early summer tan, and Josey thought with satisfaction that she looked younger than her actual forty years . . . something she had never worried about until watching her husband rolling around in bed with beautiful women on television every day at two o'clock.

Before that, being a middle-aged drama teacher at Sander's High had been just fine. In fact, the love of the theater was one of the things she and Cal had shared, but in the end it had driven them apart. She loved the stability of the small-town existence, a throwback from her childhood, while Cal had craved the excitement of the bright lights, big city.

When his evil character on *Loving Ways* was killed off the first time, Josey was secretly glad. That summer, they had both landed roles at the dinner theater in Sander's City, and Josey had fallen into the teaching job over at the high school. She had thought it was the beginning of settling into family life, but she had been wrong. New York City had lured Cal back. More often than not, he was gone on auditions, and had been ecstatic when *Loving Ways* wanted him back. Cal had wanted to move back to New York, but Josey didn't want to leave their quaint home and a job she loved for a tiny flat and an uncertain future.

With a sigh, Josey angled her head, gazing at her trim figure, which had ballooned during Cal's absence, when chocolate had become her companion. During a heated argument when Josey had commented about their lack of lovemaking, Cal had mentioned that he wasn't physically attracted to her since she had packed on the pounds. Although he had later apologized, the damage had been done.

"How will you like me now?" she wondered, with a hand on her flat tummy. After living in Cal's shadow for so long, she still wasn't entirely comfortable with her new sexy look. Her mental makeover hadn't quite caught up to her physical one. But lately, she had been feeling . . . restless, edgy, like there was something more out there for her and she needed to find it.

Josey shook her head and muttered, "Get a grip, estrogen girl," as she headed for the front door, wondering if she was having another premenopausal moment. She really didn't want Cal or her old life back, but she wouldn't be human if she didn't want him to drool just a teensy bit. To be honest, life with him hadn't been all that bad, and she had some fond memories, but his self-absorption had robbed her of her self-esteem, and she was just now getting it back. With a long sigh, Josey opened the front door, wondering if this dinner thing was a huge mistake.

Popular and trendy, Maxwell's was just a short drive away in her candy apple red Thunderbird, a midlife/postdivorce purchase that carried a big price tag but was so much more fun than her sensible blue sedan. An appreciative once-over from the twenty-something parking lot attendant had her entering the posh restaurant with her highlighted head held high.

Josey was ushered to a booth across from the elegant bar, packed full of men watching a baseball game on televisions suspended from the wall. She scooted across the plump, cushioned seat and watched for Cal to arrive.

One hour and two cosmopolitans later, Josey realized she had been stood up. For one last hopeful moment, she toyed with her cocktail napkin and watched the door for Cal's arrival. *Well, hell*, she thought, and wondered what to do. To top it all off, she was hungry, and the tantalizing aroma of grilled steak wasn't helping. Her stomach growled in protest and she remembered that the soft pretzel at the ball game was the last thing she had eaten. But sitting there dining alone was so . . . well . . . pathetic. Her nose tickled and she blinked several times, hoping to keep unwanted tears at bay. She was so damned sick of crying.

A scored run for the home team caused some commotion at the bar, but it wasn't the television that drew Josey's attention. It was the arrival of Chase Mitchell. If the man looked good in baseball pants, he looked even better in casual clothes. Close-fitting khaki slacks draped nicely over his very fine butt when he turned toward the bar to order a drink. A short-sleeved black knit shirt stretched across wide shoulders and tapered to a trim waist. There were younger, flashier men crowded around the bar, but it was Chase Mitchell who was turning female heads.

He leaned one elbow against the gleaming wooden bar while gazing up at the television, giving Josey a clear view of his profile. He had a strong jaw, high cheekbones—planes and angles softened only by the fullness of his mouth and thick, wavy brown hair.

Josey drew in a shaky breath. If she had the nerve, she would sashay up to the bar and strike up a conversation with him. After all, it wasn't as if they were complete strangers. She had come in contact with Chase on several occasions at gatherings over at Erin and Michael's house. Erin was forever singing the man's praises, telling her she should go after him.

Well, damn it, maybe she would do just that.

Josey drained the last of her cosmopolitan and licked the tart taste of lime from her lips. She smoothed her hair and took another cleansing breath. But just as she was about to scoot from the booth and make her move, a tall slinky blonde snuggled up to Chase's side and said something in his ear. He angled his head at her and laughed, flashing white teeth against his tan face.

Josey stopped in midscoot and sighed. Chase Mitchell probably didn't even remember her name. Hot moisture gathered behind her eyelids and a tear escaped. She swiped at the teardrop and looked around the dining room for her waiter. It was time to get the hell out of there.

chapter two

Chase had laughed at the blonde's slightly slurred offer to "give you the best blowjob of your life," not because he was amused, but because she had no idea how much her offer turned him off. This kind of thing came with the territory of being a pro ballplayer, but after years of fending off shallow women who wanted a piece of him for no other reason than to brag to their friends, he was glad to be coaching rather than playing.

The fame and the money had been an awesome ride, but he was more than happy to get back to just the sheer love of the game. Coaching a minor-league team meant working with guys busting their balls for a chance at the majors, giving one hundred percent each and every game. Now *that* was baseball at its best.

After turning his back on the blonde, he tilted his beer bottle up and took a long swig. Out of the corner of his eye, he caught a glimpse of Josey Cooper, the hot little friend of Erin Manning's. He knew Erin wanted to hook them up, but he also knew that Josey had gone through a painful divorce, and he didn't need a woman with baggage.

He watched her scoot to the edge of her booth, giving him a nice shot of shapely leg. She looked around the room as if searching for someone. Chase frowned. She appeared upset and that somehow managed to bother him, even though he barely knew the woman. "Baggage," he muttered under his breath, and would have turned away, but he saw her brush a tear from her cheek, and something clenched in his gut. He would bet the farm that she had been stood up.

With a soft curse, Chase pushed away from the bar, headed over to her table, and approached her. "Hello, Josey."

She blinked up at him in obvious surprise, tried to recover, and gave him a shaky smile. Her sky-blue eyes looked ready to spill a river and Chase felt another clench at his gut.

"Hello, Chase. H-how nice to see you."

God, a man could get hard just listening to her husky voice laced with a touch of Deep South. "May I join you?"

She hesitated, catching her peach-tinted bottom lip between her teeth. But then she shrugged her shoulders, deliciously bare except for two thin black straps, and waved her hand across the table. "Why the hell not, since I've been . . . stood up."

Her unexpected candor had him laughing as he slid into the booth.

"Pardon me, I don't usually curse, but I'm afraid

two cosmos on an empty stomach has loosened my tongue."

"Why, Miss Josey, you shock me," he teased, mimicking her Southern drawl.

She arched an elegant eyebrow at him. "This ole Alabama Southern belle is positively starving in more ways than one, and you, sir, look good enough to eat. I suggest you order me a meal before I slide underneath this table and have a go at you."

Okay, now he *was* shocked. Chase tried to remember the last time he was speechless. The blonde's offer of a blowjob had left him cold. Hers, however . . . did not. He tried to formulate a comeback, but all of the blood from his brain suddenly drained south.

"Look me in the eye and tell me I didn't just say that."

He could only chuckle weakly. "I'm trying to decide whether to order you food or *not*. I'm leaning towards not."

"Ah, well, I'm afraid that was the Absolut talking. Besides, I'm sure you'd be disappointed." She lifted her palms upward. "You see, my postdivorce makeover gave me a nice flat tummy and perky breasts, but deep inside, I'm just a droopy old schoolteacher. Go back to your blonde at the bar, Chase. Sex with me would be mundane in comparison."

Chase looked at her for a long moment, doubting anything with her would be mundane. His brain cried, "Baggage!" and his dick cried, "Sex!" In the end, it was the fact that he found her so damned likable that made him stay. "Josey, I didn't come to Maxwell's for sex. I came here for a cold beer and a hot, juicy steak. Now, care to join me?"

A slow smile spread across her face. "I do believe I will."

"Good," he said, and meant it. "Can I order you another drink?"

She held up her martini glass with a wince. "No, thank you. My lips are loose enough."

Her statement brought his attention to her mouth. Her lips looked shiny and soft, and he told himself before the night was over he was going to kiss that lush mouth of hers. "Well, then, let's order dinner."

He ordered steak and she opted for sea bass, and he noticed that although she used things like sour cream and butter sparingly, she wasn't afraid to eat. That pleased him. He hated dining with a woman who was afraid of food. Throughout the meal, he found there wasn't much about her that *didn't* please him. He especially enjoyed the fact that she loved baseball.

"So, how long have you lived in Sander's City?" Chase asked as he reached for his water glass. "It's obvious from your accent that you didn't grow up in the Midwest."

"I did my student teaching here, oh, about fifteen years ago and came back several times to do summer theater. When the job for the drama teacher opened up I snatched it while my ex-husband directed the dinner theater. I moved here for good three years ago." She tilted her head and gave him a smile. "But you're right—I grew up in a tiny town in Alabama just north of the Florida border. My daddy owned an open-air market, selling boiled peanuts and peaches to the folks heading to the Panhandle for vacation."

Chase wrinkled his nose. "Boiled peanuts?"

Josey grinned. "It's an acquired taste."

"Like grits?"

"Hey, don't you go making fun of grits, the food of the gods, Mr. Deep-Dish Pizza."

Chase raised his eyebrows. "You can tell I'm from Chicago?"

Josey raised her hands palms up. "Why is it that people think the only Americans with an accent are from the South?"

Chase leaned forward. "I think your soft Southern drawl is sexy as hell," he said, and was surprised when her blue eyes rounded. In the dim light of the restaurant, he could still tell that she was blushing as if she didn't realize how damned alluring she truly was. Since she seemed a bit uncomfortable, he backed off and changed the subject. "So, how did you come to be such a baseball fan?"

She grinned and seemed more at ease. "That was about all there was to do where I grew up. We had one small movie theater and a dozen baseball parks." She shrugged, drawing his attention to the delicate curve of her shoulders. "I'm one of the few women who, when she hears the word *diamond,* thinks of a baseball field."

"Good God, woman, where have you been all my life?" Chase meant the statement as a joke, but their eyes met across the table and the moment seemed suspended. A bit shaken, Chase cleared his throat. "So . . . you come to the Flyers games often?"

She nodded. "I have season tickets with Erin Manning. Our mutual love of the game is what initially made my relationship with Erin go beyond that of principal and teacher," Josey explained, and then grinned. "I still can't get over the fact that she and Michael Manning are married and soon to be parents."

Chase swallowed a bite of steak and then shook his head. "Damn, he was a great pitcher. It was a shame he had to bust up his leg."

"I agree." She dabbed at her mouth with her napkin. "Life is unpredictable. But a bad situation can turn into a good one in the end if you let it." She gave him a soft smile and the lift of one eyebrow. "Like getting stood up."

"Any man who would stand you up is a fool."

"Chase Mitchell, you have me melting like sugar in hot tea. Damn, but you're good for a girl's ego."

"I only speak the truth."

"Would you like to stop back at my house for some coffee or an after-dinner drink?"

"That would be nice."

"Great. I promise to turn on ESPN so we can catch the play of the day."

Chase leaned forward and took her hand in his. "I don't need any incentive other than your company."

"Oh, my God, you're good."

It wasn't a come-on. He really enjoyed her company, but he wasn't ready to let her know how fast he was falling under her spell. "Girl, you ain't seen nothin' yet."

She laughed, and he wasn't about to let on that he was serious as hell.

chapter
three

Josey glanced in her rearview mirror for the tenth time, sure that the black BMW Chase was driving would suddenly make a U-turn instead of following her home. She felt excited . . . no, make that nervous *and* more sexually keyed up than she had been in a long, long time.

Josey let out a shaky sigh. She wanted him to kiss her, hold her. "Oh, be honest," she chided herself. "You want the man to fuck your brains out."

The problem was, she had never really had her brains fucked out, whatever that meant. Cal had been a very me-on-top-in-bed kinda guy. Josey moaned. She just bet Chase was one of those give-it-to-you-in-every-room lovers. Up against the wall, halfway up the stairs because he couldn't wait to get into the bedroom. She imagined his mouth on her in places where Cal had never gone and moaned again. She had wondered once if Cal was gay, but she soon realized that he just hated anything . . . sweaty. Sex with him was neat and orderly with little mess. He had looked at her in horror once when she had suggested slathering each other with whipped cream and chocolate sauce.

Unfortunately, Cal's obsession with his career had led to Josey's *consuming* too much whipped cream and chocolate, making sex go from neat and tidy to not at all. An overweight wife for Cal Cooper was not an option. God, she thought about the big sexy man following her home and felt totally overwhelmed. *This couldn't be happening.*

Josey inhaled a deep, shaky breath and blew it out, trying to gain her composure as she pulled into the driveway of her small brick town house. Before she was totally self-contained, Chase opened her car door and offered his hand.

"I like this section of town," Chase commented as they strolled up the brick paved walk to her front door. "These homes have a lot of character that you won't find in something new."

Josey angled her head at him and smiled, glad to find another thing in common. "I agree, but I have to warn you. The interior is a work in progress."

They were almost to the front door when a shadowy figure suddenly stood up from the porch. Josey gasped and clutched Chase's arm but then realized the man was none other than Cal Cooper.

"Well, what have we here?" Cal asked, the irritation in his voice clear.

Josey felt the tension in Chase's arm and cringed. Cal loved to create a scene, and Josey had no doubt that Chase wouldn't hesitate to deck her arrogant ex.

"Chase is a friend. He joined me for dinner when you failed to show up."

"Baby, I'm sorry. My plane was late." He looked her over from head to toe. "You look amazing, by the way. You've lost weight."

Yeah, about one hundred and sixty pounds of it that had been hanging around my neck, she thought with a small smile. Oh, how she had wanted to impress him, and now she just wanted him gone. "You could have called," Josey accused, and felt a horrible sense of déjà vu. What in the hell was she doing? This man was gone . . . *gone* from her life and for damned good reasons. "I'm sorry, Cal, but you need to leave."

"I thought I could crash at your place." He flicked Chase a look. "On the sofa, of course." His lingering glance at Josey suggested otherwise.

"I think Josey made her request clear. You need to leave."

"And I think this is none of your business."

Josey swallowed nervously. You could cut the cloud of testosterone with a knife. "Cal, you really need to go," she pleaded softly. *And never come back.*

"Baby, I said I was sorry."

"Cal, that's a tired old tune that I never want to hear again. This whole dinner thing was a mistake."

"Josey"—he took a step toward her—"you don't mean that."

"She means it," Chase said firmly.

"Butt out, Buster," Cal sneered, and poked a finger in Chase's direction.

"Did you just call me *Buster*?" Chase chuckled without real mirth. "Put that finger away before I—"

"Chase, don't." Josey put a restraining hand on his chest. He glanced down at her, giving Cal the opportunity to take a swing. Josey screamed when Cal's fist clipped Chase's jaw, sending him staggering backwards.

"You stupid son of a bitch." Chase took a threatening step forward.

Cal's eyes widened as if he just realized this was real life, and not a soap opera scene. He backpedaled with his hands in the air. "Hey, man, I'm sorry. I was out of line."

Chase rubbed his jaw. "Get the fuck out of here or they'll have to scrape your sorry ass off the concrete."

"Josey—" Cal began.

"I know, Cal. You're sorry."

Chase took a step in his direction.

"I'm going."

Josey turned to Chase. "I'm so sorry. I'll understand if you want to leave."

"No way. I want that asshole to see my car parked in front of your place. I don't even want him to think of coming back," he growled, but then lowered his voice. "Besides, I want to spend some more time with you."

Josey rummaged in her purse for her door key. "You're sure?"

He tucked his finger underneath her chin, forcing her to look up at him. "Positive."

She made a sound halfway between a sigh of relief and a nervous laugh as she opened the door. A flick of the light switch bathed the living room with a soft glow. Josey swept her hand toward the caramel-colored leather sofa angled toward a big-screen television. "The remote is on the coffee table. I'll put on a pot of decaf and then I'm getting out of this dress."

He grinned. "Need any help?"

"Making the coffee?"

"No, the getting-out-of-the-dress part."

Josey felt heat creep into her cheeks. "I didn't mean—"

Chase chuckled and took a step closer to her. "I'm just playing. Relax, Josey."

"I'm trying, but I'm not very good at this sort of thing."

He frowned. "What sort of thing?"

She raised her palms upward. "Entertaining a man like you in my home."

His frown deepened, but she saw amusement in his brown eyes. "A man like me? Just what is a man like me, Josey?"

"Confident, successful, experienced, and sexy enough to make my knees weak. You're just a little too much for this small-town schoolteacher to handle."

"I'm just a small-town ballplayer."

"Oh, please, you're—" she began, but he cut her protest off with a kiss that made her melt like saltwater taffy.

"I've wanted to do that since the first day I laid eyes on you last summer over at the high school."

"In Erin's office?"

"Yeah." He nuzzled her neck and kissed her bare shoulder.

"Y-you remember that day?" Oh, God, he was sending shivers down her spine. His lips were so warm and he smelled so damned good.

"Yeah, and you have box seats behind our dugout. Today you were wearing white shorts and a blue halter top."

"So what took you"—she gasped when his mouth found the swell of her breast—"so long to approach me?"

"Erin told me you were going through a divorce and quite frankly, I didn't want to get tangled up in that mess."

"And do you want to get tangled up with me *now*?"

He pulled her against him and she could feel the heat, the steely hardness, of his erection. "What do you think?"

"I think I will disappoint you."

"And why exactly is that?"

"I'm not very good in . . . you know . . . *bed*."

Chase hated the look of uncertainty in her expressive blue eyes. That asshole ex-husband of hers should be shot. Right now Chase sorely regretted not pounding Cal's sorry ass into the ground. He was going to show Josey Cooper just how good she could be. "Well, now, then we won't do it in bed."

"That's not what I mea—"

He smothered her stupid protest with his mouth, gently coaxing, probing, until she surrendered with a moan deep in her throat. She wrapped her arms around his neck and leaned into his embrace.

Chase threaded his fingers into her silky hair and deepened the kiss. Tongues tangled, danced. He couldn't get enough of her . . . couldn't get close enough. With his teeth, he tugged the black straps of her dress over her shoulders, giving him better access to the soft swell of her breasts. He buried his face there, inhaling her sweet perfume.

With one quick move, he unzipped her dress and let it glide to the floor, and then untangled her arms from his neck. "Let me look at you."

"No . . . I'm—"

"You're gorgeous," he said, and meant it. She stood before him wearing only a black satin strapless bra, next-to-nothing black panties, high heels, and pearls. He backed her up against the wall and kissed her lips, her neck, her belly, and then nuzzled his mouth between her legs. He could feel her moist heat beneath the black silk. Inhaling deeply, his head reeled from the subtle scent of her floral perfume mingled with the musk of a woman. With a growl, he hooked his fingers into the side of her panties and tugged.

She gasped in protest. "Chase, please . . . no!"

He ignored her plea, hooked one of her legs over his shoulder, and supported her with his other hand. He leaned into her and licked her vulva oh so lightly.

She shivered and clutched at his shoulders. "God, *Chase.*"

He licked her labia again and again until she was throbbing, pulsing beneath his eager mouth. With his shoulders, he nudged her thighs open wider and then entered her slick folds with his tongue, going deep. God, she was so hot, so sweet, filling his head with her scent, her taste, driving him wild. He moved his tongue in and out, in and out until her thighs quivered and her breath came in short gasps. Knowing she was close, he suddenly lifted her other leg over his shoulder, held her ass with both of his open palms, pinning her against the wall while he opened her sex wide.

When she arched up, he licked her hard . . . *harder*, nipping and then sucking on her swollen clit. With a gasp, she suddenly blossomed beneath his mouth, and then cried out his name. With a contented groan, he slid his tongue inside, feeling her clutch as she rode out the orgasm.

chapter four

Josey felt like a rag doll . . . all floppy and heavy-limbed. Chase's muscles quivered and she realized he was holding up all of her weight. "Y-you can put me down," she said gruffly into his ear.

"Hold on to me, baby," he answered.

She clung to him as he carried her over to the sofa. The butter-soft leather felt cool against her heated skin, making her shiver. For a moment she simply blinked up at him, stunned and tingling all over.

And then it began to slowly sink in that she was nearly naked and she had let him do . . . God . . . *that*. She felt the heat of a full-body blush and tried to sit up, but her shaky limbs wouldn't cooperate.

"Oh, no, you don't," Chase said, and put a restraining hand on her belly. "I'm not nearly done with you."

"Chase, I . . . we . . . shouldn't do this."

He knelt down beside the sofa. "Give me a good

reason why not and I'll back off. And don't give me that 'You'll be disappointed' baloney."

Josey took a deep breath. "I'm still not used to the new made-over me. Like I told you, I lost some weight, had a little work done, and, well, basically did myself over."

Chase chuckled. "Looking good is the best revenge?"

Josey nodded. "Something like that."

"So, what are you telling me?" He rocked back on his heels and waited.

Josey licked her lips and tried to find the words to explain, but her brain was still a bit befuddled by the mind-blowing orgasm. "Well, what you see isn't exactly what you get." She pursed her lips. "And it sort of irks me that you wouldn't have given me the time of day before the, ah, new me."

"Oh, get off your high horse."

"Pardon me?" She pushed up to her elbows.

"Would I be here if I looked like Tommy Lasorda?"

"What?"

"It works two ways, baby. A beer gut wouldn't have gotten you out of that dress."

"Women aren't like that."

"Bullshit. Let me tell you something. I've had women throw themselves at me just because I was a pro ballplayer and they wanted to get laid by someone famous."

Josey pushed up to a sitting position and they were suddenly nose to nose. "Are you accusing *me* of wanting you because of who you are?" she sputtered. God, she had had enough of arrogant men!

He shrugged, causing her to sputter again. "Why you arrogant . . . you . . . you!" She shoved at his shoulders, trying to think of something vile enough to call him.

Chase caught her wrists in his hands and then asked quietly, "Why did you invite me over here?"

Her chin came up. "I like you."

He cocked an eyebrow at her.

"Okay, *okay!* I find you insanely attractive too. You have the best doggone butt ever to grace a pair of baseball pants. There. Are you happy?"

"Oh, not just yet." He tugged his shirt over his head.

"Wh-what are you doing?" Josey's heart skipped a beat.

"Getting naked."

"Why?"

"I think you know the answer to that question, Josey. I just hope like hell you have protection."

"Protection?"

"A rubber."

"Oh, a condom." She chewed on her bottom lip. Did she have a condom somewhere? She scrambled from the sofa, snatched up his discarded shirt to cover her near nakedness, and hurried to the bathroom.

Josey opened the sink cabinet and pushed past a variety of stuff. No condom. Then she snapped her fingers. Oh, yeah. Cal used to keep some in the top drawer of the nightstand. She hurried down the short hallway to her bedroom and yanked open the small drawer. Bingo. There were several. She picked one up, held it in the palm of her hand, and stared at it. In the heat of the moment she would—okay, she *did*—let Chase do whatever he wanted to do with that magic mouth of his. But now . . . now the moment was gone she felt . . . God, what did she feel?

Petrified. Yeah, that was the word.

She stood there rooted to the carpet for God knows how long, staring at the foil packet in her palm.

"Josey?"

With a little squeal, she jumped and dropped the condom.

"Ah, you found one. Good."

Josey nodded, leaned over to pick up the condom, and then turned to face him. Oh, God. He was stark naked and—ohmygod. Huge.

The man had a . . . *dick* like a baseball bat.

"Y-you could hit a home run with that thing."

He grinned. "I plan on getting at least past first base."

Josey swallowed. "You are rather large, aren't you?"

He shrugged. "Big hands, big feet . . ."

She frowned. "Big penis?"

"Something like that. Geez, Josey, I'm not *that* big. Just aroused. Believe me, I'll fit."

"I'm nervous as hell." She swallowed a hysterical giggle. Maybe Cal had just been really small?

Chase approached her, led by his bobbing penis. "I'm *hard* as hell."

"You're not making this any easier." Her heart thumped wildly and she backed up. The back of her legs hit the mattress and she plopped down weakly on the edge of the bed.

"How about this?" he offered gently. "*You* are in control. I'll lie down on this bed and you can do with me as you please. You set the pace and we'll take it from there."

"Chase, I told you! I'm no good at this."

"Right," he commented, drawing out the word.

Josey took a deep breath and stood up. "Okay, lie down."

He did, looking ridiculously masculine surrounded by frilly pillows on the floral bedspread. The only light on in the room was the small lamp on the nightstand, leaving the room bathed with a soft glow.

"Join me," he said, and patted the mattress. "And stop wringing your hands."

Josey nodded. "Okay." She climbed onto the bed and knelt beside him. "Now what?"

"Whatever you want."

She bobbed her head again. "I think I'll just look for a minute or two. Is that okay?"

"Yeah. But don't be afraid to touch."

Josey swallowed and then wet her dry lips with the tip of her tongue. Just *looking* at him was getting her hot. She realized at that moment that her sensual side had just gotten a wake-up call. Big-time. He had wide, wide shoulders, nicely defined pecs covered lightly with tawny hair. And he had the hard, honed body of an athlete. Cal had been lean and trim, attractive in his own way, but Chase was . . . God, *virile*, rugged.

And he was hers to play with all night long. Ahh . . . where to begin?

She tentatively reached over and trailed her fingers over the silky, springy hair on his chest. His skin was warm, smooth. She swirled her fingertip over his nipple and then down over his ridged stomach, brushing lightly against the jutting length of his erection.

He inhaled sharply, drawing her attention to his face. Ahh . . . that face. No pretty boy here. Fine lines around his brown eyes, a thin scar on his chin, and a slightly crooked nose, presumably from a break, showed that he played long and hard. Dark stubble shadowed the strong line of his jaw. Oh, yeah, he was all man.

"Mmmmm." With that soft sound in the back of her throat, Josey traced his mouth with her fingertip. He had full, sculpted lips that she knew firsthand could work magic on a woman. Chase Mitchell might be a hard-muscled tough guy, but his beautiful mouth begged to be kissed.

And so she did. Letting her tongue replace her fingertip, she leaned forward and licked his full bottom lip before kissing him softly. But when he opened his mouth for more, she left him wanting.

"Josey—"

She put her index finger to his mouth. "Hush. Let me get acquainted with this big beautiful body of yours." Part of her was buying time while she worked up the nerve to actually have sex with him. Plus, suddenly having this man that she had ogled for the past month was a gift she wanted to savor and enjoy.

And so she did, inch by glorious inch. Soon,

though, nervousness gave way to trembling desire, chasing away the I-can't-believe-I'm-doing-this fear. The sound of his moan near her ear made her shiver, *tingle*, and then go hot all over. Her nipples tightened and she grew incredibly wet with wanting him, needing him . . . buried deep inside her.

chapter five

Sweet Jesus, thought Chase. She was driving him insane. What in the hell was he thinking? He should be fucking her senseless by now instead of letting her slowly torture him. He groaned when she abandoned his needy mouth, trailing her tongue over his chin. She paused to nuzzle his neck and then suck his earlobe, sending his dick into orbit.

His big shirt hid Josey's nakedness from his view, but the brush of her soft skin against him reminded him of the fact. "Ditch the shirt," he pleaded.

"Hmm?" She paused in her close examination of his chest and gave him a smile. "I feel like this is Christmas morning and I've been a very good girl."

"Josey, now is the time to get your name on the naughty list."

She responded with a throaty laugh and cupped his balls. "Nice package. Missing a bow, though."

"Baby, you look good in my shirt, but ditch the damn thing. I want to see you naked."

"Oh."

For a moment he thought she was going to refuse. But then she tugged his black shirt over her head.

"The bra too." He had yet to see her breasts.

Her hands shook, but she unhooked the front clasp, letting her tumble free. "I'm not very . . . *big*."

The apology in her voice made him smile. "But you're perky."

"You're making fun of me."

"Josey?"

"Yes?"

"Let me put one of those perky breasts in my mouth."

"I told you I'm not very good at this." Her mouth puckered into a pout.

If he hadn't seen the tremble in her hands and the wariness in her blue eyes, he would have suspected that she was screwing with him. "Josey, put your hand around my *baseball bat* and tell me what you feel."

With her bottom lip caught between her teeth, she scooted over, *holy cow*, straddled his thighs, and wrapped her hand around his shaft. "It's, well . . . very hard."

"Exactly," he said through gritted teeth. "You must be doing something right."

"Oh."

"Josey?"

"Yes?" Her voice dropped an octave and she looked down at him through half-lidded eyes with her hand still clutching his cock.

"Slip the condom on me and show me just how very bad you are in bed."

She looked at him for one long moment and then gave him a trembling smile. "No complaining, you hear me?"

"Don't worry."

He watched her open the packet with her teeth. Frowning in cute concentration, she carefully rolled the condom onto his painfully hard dick.

"Y-you want me to be on top?"

"You set the pace, remember?"

"Chase—"

"Baby, you can do this. Go as slow or as fast as you want. Just please. Do it!"

She nodded and then scooted up until she straddled him around the waist. He could feel her moist heat. With a breathy little gasp, she splayed her palms on his chest and then rubbed against his erection.

"I need to kiss you first," she whispered as she leaned forward, and then placed her lips against his.

"Not a problem," Chase murmured against her mouth. He wrapped his arms around her but let her take the lead. The kiss, gentle at first, quickly deepened. She rocked against him, rubbing her breasts against his chest.

Chase couldn't stand it any longer. He had to be inside her. He rose up into a half-sitting position against the pile of pillows. His hands found her waist, lifted her up, and guided her to the tip of his oh-so-ready cock. Their eyes met and she nodded.

With a little whimper, she let him sink into her heat inch by inch until he filled her completely. With her knees on either side of his hips and her hands on his shoulders, she slowly rose up and then sank back down, easing his hard length almost out and then slowly back in.

Chase gritted his teeth with the effort of holding back. He wanted to flip her over and fuck her hard and fast, but this was her show and it was obvious it had been a while since she had performed. God, she was tight. With a moan, he dipped his head and caught one pebbled nipple in his mouth, swirling his tongue and then nipping with his teeth.

With a gasp, she arched her back, came up onto her knees and then quickly back down, driving him into her hard.

"God, Josey!"

"Help me," she pleaded. "I—want to go faster, but my legs are . . . are like Jell-O."

Chase needed no other encouragement. Encircling her waist with his hands, he lifted her up, guiding her, helping her go faster, harder. His breath came in quick gasps while blood pounded in his ears. She leaned forward, digging her fingers into his shoulders, moving up and then slamming down. God, she felt so tight, so slick, so hot. . . .

And then she threw back her head and cried out, "Chase!"

The ragged cry of his name on her lips swept him right along with her. Pleasure exploded in his brain. Her orgasm squeezed him, milked every last drop from him until he fell weakly back against the pillows, taking her with him.

Hearts thudding, they remained tangled and

breathing hard. "My God," Chase finally managed, and chuckled weakly. "Yeah, baby, you're really bad at this. If you were any worse, I think I'd be dead."

She pushed slightly up from his chest and angled her head at him. "Really?"

"Oh, come on. I think I've been had."

"Huh?"

"You ever heard of a pool shark?"

She giggled low in her throat. "You mean a guy who pretends to be bad and then really isn't?"

"Yeah. Well, I think you're a sex shark."

"Mmmm, so *not* true." She gave him a warm smile. "I think it has something to do with who I'm with. But you were right about one thing. You have been thoroughly *had*." She leaned forward and kissed him. "And I intend to have you again and again and . . . again."

⁓ chapter
six

Two hours and three condoms later, Josey was so sated she could hardly move. With a satisfied groan she untangled her happy self from his embrace and scooted to the side of the bed. "How about some dessert?"

He moaned. "Can you give me a minute?"

Josey chuckled. "I mean food, like in the form of ice cream."

"Oh . . . sure," he said with a tired wave of his hand. "Ice cream."

"I'll be back in a jiffy," she promised, and pulled on his black shirt once again.

"Like I'm able to go anywhere."

Josey stumbled into the kitchen and opened the freezer. After heaping a bowl full of mint chocolate chip, she made her way back to her bedroom.

She paused in the doorway just to look at him. The pillows had long ago been scattered to the floor and the covers turned back. With his eyes closed, Chase leaned against the headboard, arms folded behind his head. The white sheet pooled around his waist, exposing his wide tanned chest, washboard abs, and one long leg.

She grinned. The poor man looked plumb tuckered out. But then she swallowed. And good enough to eat. Not wanting to wake him, Josey scooted quietly onto the mattress and took a big bite of minty ice cream.

"Hey, aren't you going to share?"

The deep, sexy voice had her melting faster than the ice cream in her mouth. With a smile, she twisted toward him with a spoonful of the dessert. He leaned forward and took the offered bite.

"Mmmm. Tastes almost as good as you."

She arched an eyebrow at him. "Oh, really?" Setting the bowl aside, she rose up onto her knees and gave him a long mint-flavored kiss.

"I stand corrected. Nothing tastes as good as you."

"You sure are good for a girl's ego," Josey told him with a smile.

Chase frowned at her. "Do you think I'm handing you a line?"

Her smile faded as she retrieved the bowl and swirled her spoon in the ice cream. "I'm not sure what to think. I barely know you."

He tucked a finger under her chin and she was forced to look at him. "I'd like to change that, but first I want you to be honest with me."

"Okay."

"Are you over your ex?"

Josey sighed. "I'm not in love with him, if that's what you're asking."

"That's what I'm asking."

Josey took a bite of the ice cream, giving herself a moment to think. She felt more relaxed, sexier, than she had ever felt with Cal, but she felt odd saying that to him.

"I'm sorry. I'm pushing."

Josey was surprised that he sounded insecure . . . worried. She felt a tingle of excitement. Did this mean he had feelings for her? But then she remembered the leggy blonde that was all over him at the bar and another thought hit her hard. This guy was a chick magnet. Falling in love with him would be setting herself up for another heartbreak.

"Josey?" he asked gently. "What is going on in that pretty head of yours?"

"A couple of things that I probably shouldn't tell you."

He sat up straight. "Tell me."

Josey took a deep breath and blew it out. "Okay. First of all, sex with you was mind-blowing. I was married for five years and never once did Cal make me feel the way that you did today. That tells me what I suspected all along. Cal and I were much better friends than lovers."

He grinned. "Well, it was my pleasure to set you straight." His grin faded when she frowned. "Oh, this is when you send me packing."

"I—I just can't get involved with someone like you."

His dark eyebrows rose. "Someone like me?"

The slight anger in his tone had her shaking her head. "Chase—"

"No, I get it. You think I'm the stereotypical pro athlete fucking every woman in sight." He waved his hand across the rumpled bed. "Do you think that's what *this* was all about?"

"No, I—"

"Well, then, I have a proposition for you." He tried to scramble from the bed, but his long legs got all twisted up in the sheet. He wound up falling over the edge of the bed, landing hard. "Fuck!"

Josey crept over to the side of the bed and peeked cautiously down at him. He was kicking furiously at the sheet, getting even more tangled in the process. "Fuck, fuck . . . *fuck!*"

"You, ah, need some—"

"No!" He gave up his fight with the sheet. "Just listen. Tomorrow night after the game, I want to take you out to dinner."

"A date?"

"Yes."

Josey frowned. "So what is the proposition?"

"No sex."

Josey looked down at him. God, he looked so delicious . . . all naked, angry, and rumpled. The sheet revealed more skin than it covered. She swallowed. "What exactly do you mean?"

"You heard me. No sex. We'll have dinner." He shrugged. "Maybe a movie. I'll show you that there is much more to Chase Mitchell than—"

"Your baseball bat?" She struggled not to smile.

He gave the sheet another kick. "Exactly."

Josey nodded, trying desperately not to laugh. The tables had somehow gotten turned in this whole thing. He had nothing to prove. She already knew there was much more to him than sex, and his caring, giving nature in bed was a dead giveaway.

He had missed her whole point. If she had thought there was nothing more to him than his *baseball bat*, she would have no problem with seeing him. A hot little fling was something she could handle. It was the falling-in-love thing that had her spooked.

But she would never give him that bit of ammo. Oh, no, let him think the whole problem was based on her shallow opinion of him. "You'll never be able to do it, Chase, so let's not try, okay?"

"Don't you think I at least deserve a chance?"

Josey wasn't prepared for that argument. Fairness was something she taught to her students, a code that she lived by. She sighed. "Yes, you deserve a chance."

He grinned up at her, looking so pleased that her heart melted. She would just have to make sure that he failed on his no-sex mission.

chapter
seven

The next day, Chase glanced up into the stands and knew his ridiculous no-sex plan was already in jeopardy. Josey gave him an oh-so-innocent wave of her fingers, but he was on to her. He should have realized that she wouldn't make this stupid proposal easy, and she was dressed for battle. A yellow straw hat shaded her eyes and she wore an off-the-shoulder sundress of the same soft buttery color. Hot damn. Only a Southern woman could wear a hat like that and mean it.

Chase tipped his ball cap at Josey and Erin before entering the dugout and plopping down on the bench. He went over his lineup without really thinking about it. He was thinking about *her* looking cool as a cucumber when he was already sweating. He uncapped a sports drink and took a long guzzle. "I'll show you," he grumbled, drawing a curious glance from the batboy. "I won't give in."

He grinned as he signaled for his new pitcher, Reese Taylor, to warm up. A southpaw, and he had a sweet curveball. Yeah, this kid was a hotshot that had potential. But as he watched, his thoughts drifted to the evening he had strategically planned. First he would pick up a picnic basket from a fancy deli full of stuff he wouldn't like—wine, Brie, fruit, pâté—but that *she* would. Next on his hidden agenda was listening to a symphony pops concert in the park while lounging on a blanket with the picnic basket.

"Ha!" he said, drawing the attention of the batboy again. Classy. Romantic. By the end of the night she would be so hot for him, she wouldn't be able to stand it.

And he would give her a swift peck on the cheek at her door, leaving her so frustrated that she wouldn't get one minute of sleep for thinking of him! Now *that* was a plan. And by God, he was sticking to it even if it killed him.

During the national anthem, Chase sneaked another glance up at Josey. He could see that she was singing, and that somehow pleased him. A sudden balmy breeze caused her to grasp at her hat and skirt which billowed upward, giving him a good look at her long legs and, holy shit . . . a thong? The woman was wearing a thong?

The anthem ended, but Chase remained rooted to the spot with his hat over his heart. Josey angled her head in his direction and even though the big hat shaded her eyes, he could feel the warmth of her gaze upon him. Her mouth, wearing some shiny shade of red, curved upward in a sultry smile that made his heart thud, pumping blood straight to his dick. With a groan, he headed for the cover of the dugout before he got a boner in his tight baseball pants.

Trying to concentrate on the game, Chase leaned against the railing and watched the play begin. Once again, his young pitcher Reese Taylor was pitching an impressive game. By the end of the seventh inning, he had a two-hit shutout going and was still looking strong.

Chase stood up and leaned against the railing. Reese had the batter at three balls and two strikes. With a shake of his head he shook off the catcher's sign and then nodded his agreement. Winding up, Reese threw a high hard fastball, impossible to hit and impossible for the batter to resist. Swing and a miss. Hot damn, he was good.

"The kid's got what it takes," commented Jack Kingman, the pitching coach. "You thinking 'bout sending him up?"

"Not yet. He's got some maturing to do. Just last week in Akron, I had to pull him out of a bar fight. He's got super control on the mound, but is wild off the field." Chase spit in the dirt and then shook his head.

"I heard the other guy made a racial slur, Chase. Can you blame him for taking a swing?"

Chase shrugged. "Look, I know his upbringing wasn't easy, but he's got to get rid of that damn chip on his shoulder. That shit won't fly in the majors."

"Yeah, but—"

Chase raised a hand to cut Jack off. "I know you like him, but he's not going anywhere until he gets his act together. You can tell him I said so."

Jack nodded. "Gotcha."

"Hey, I'm sorry for being such a hard-ass. I'm a little on edge."

Jack chuckled. "Got anything to do with the lady in the yellow dress?"

"How in the hell did you know that?"

"You keep gawking at her."

"Shit."

Jack nudged him with his elbow. "You gonna ask her out?"

"I'm having dinner with her after the game."

"So . . . you gonna take the edge *off*?"

Chase swallowed a moan when he thought about his stupid fucking . . . no, make that *not*-fucking plan. "I plan on being the perfect gentleman."

Jack snorted and slapped his hat against his thigh. "Yeah, right."

"Hey, I'm serious."

"Yeah, yeah. Just tell me tomorrow how good she was, okay?"

"Don't talk about her like that."

Jack held his hands up in the air. "Sorry. I was just kidding around."

"Well, don't."

"You like her that much?"

Chase felt a sudden jolt at the question, which sizzled in his brain, and sank lower. "Yeah, I guess I do."

"Well, hot damn. I've known you for fifteen years and it's finally happening."

"What?"

"You're falling in love." Jack drew out the word *love* and then hooted.

Chase gave him a shove and would have argued, but the inning suddenly ended with a pop fly ball to the shortstop. "We need some runs," he bellowed as the infield filed into the dugout. "Reese," he said, grabbing him, "I'm gonna pinch-hit for you."

"I can finish the game."

Chase shook his head. "We need to score some runs. Jack, get Mitch warming up to close this thing."

Jack nodded.

Chase held his tongue when Reese slammed his mitt to the ground with an oath. The kid needed an attitude adjustment, but he understood his anger at being pulled, so he let it slide. His thoughts turned to Josey and he sighed. Jack's crack about him screwing her had him fuming, and he wondered if his friend was right. Could he be falling in love?

There was a time when the thought of falling in love would have scared him shitless. But lately, he had thoughts of settling down. Maybe it was the small-town living or the happiness he saw between Michael and Erin. He chuckled. Or maybe he was just getting old.

He knew one thing for sure. Josey Cooper was one hell of a woman and keeping his hands off of her was going to be tough.

Josey stood up for the seventh-inning stretch. As much as she loved baseball, this game seemed to be taking forever.

"I'm hungry," Erin announced for the third time that afternoon.

"And let me guess. You have to pee."

"Yes. Want to come with me?"

Josey nodded. "I could use a frozen lemonade." She eyed her pregnant friend. "And maybe you should get out of this heat for a little while."

"Sounds good to me. We can watch an inning on the indoor television screen."

After a quick stop in the ladies' room, they headed for the lounge. They ordered drinks and a snack and found a booth.

"So tell me, have you slept with Chase Mitchell?"

Josey almost choked on her lemonade slushy. She swallowed the Gulp too quickly and had brain freeze.

"Oh, my God. You have."

Josey cleared her throat. "He treated me to dinner when Cal failed to show."

Erin ground her teeth together. "That jerk."

Twirling her straw in her drink, Josey said, "The weird thing was, Cal showed up at the house and caught me with Chase."

"He didn't catch you, Josey. You're divorced."

"I know. It just felt . . . strange. The even stranger part was that Cal acted jealous."

"Oh, Josey—"

She held up her hand. "Don't worry. Being with Chase made me realize . . ."

"What?" Erin leaned in close. "Oh, come on. Don't leave me hanging."

Josey looked at Erin. "The man positively makes me melt. Cal never, *ever* made me feel like that."

Erin was so excited she ignored her food. "So are you going to see Chase again?"

"I'm having dinner with him tonight," Josey said glumly.

Erin frowned. "You don't sound too pleased about it."

"I'm not," she said, and took a long drink of her lemonade. "The only reason I agreed is because he promised to keep his hands to himself."

"Now, why would you want him to do that?"

"Because I don't feel like setting myself up for a fall, that's why."

Erin tucked a lock of red hair behind her ear and gave Josey a long, hard look.

"What?"

"You know, right after your divorce and your makeover madness, you marched into my office with not only a brand-new look, but a new attitude. You seemed ready to take on the world."

Josey sighed. "Yeah, and then reality sank in. Forty years old, dumped, and lonely. Kinda took away my bravado."

"So do you want your old life back?"

"You mean with Cal?"

"Yes."

"No. He's not the jerk you think he is, but no, I don't want him or my old life back."

"Then get your groove back, girlfriend. Go for this thing with Chase. Have some fun."

"I'm afraid, Erin. He's a hellava lot of man for this old schoolteacher to handle. Do you seriously think I could hold the attention of a man like Chase?"

"You mean a famous, former major-league baseball player that women drool over?"

Josey nodded.

"And you think he's—pardon the pun—out of your league?"

She nodded again.

Erin gave her a deadpan stare. "Been there. Thought that. And almost lost Michael because of it. Give the man a fighting chance."

Josey swallowed the fear bubbling up in her throat and tried to smile.

"Oh, come on. Show me some at-ti-tude." Erin broke down the syllables and gave her a sassy head bop.

With a giggle, Josey raised her slushy in the air. "Here's to my new attitude." They clunked plastic cups.

"You're a great friend, Erin. Have I told you that lately?"

Erin sniffed and swiped at a tear. "I'm sorry. I cry at everything. Greeting-card commercials make me bawl. It drives Michael crazy."

Josey reached across the plastic table and patted Erin on the arm. "Michael is going to make a wonderful daddy. I've seen him in action with his niece."

Erin sniffed loudly and another fat tear escaped. "Oh, stop!" she said with a watery giggle and then gave Josey a high five. "Chase Mitchell will never know what hit him."

chapter eight

Chase stunned the locker room full of half-naked men when he gave them a tip of his hat and a snappy "Good game" instead of his usual postgame speech. Eager to be with Josey, he took a quick shower and changed into khakis and a blue golf shirt. He had asked her to wait for him in the lounging area just outside his office. Taking a deep breath, he reminded himself to keep his hands off of her, and then opened the door.

She looked up from the couch, where she sat flipping through a *Sports Illustrated*, and smiled. "Good game, coach."

He shrugged. "Pitchers' duel. Those low scoring games can be boring." He crossed the small room, which smelled of her perfume, and politely extended his hand.

She hesitated, but then grasped his hand and rose to

her feet. "I wasn't bored one bit. Just watching Reese Taylor is enough fun for me."

"The kid's got what it takes. Just needs to settle down." Chase knew he should let go of her hand, but he liked the feel of her small hand in his, and holding hands was innocent enough, wasn't it? He pushed open the door and they walked down the narrow hallway leading to the back entrance, where his car was parked.

"I hope you're hungry," he said as he opened the door of his black BMW.

"A little." She slid into the leather seat, giving him an enticing show of tan leg. She grinned up at him. "But Erin tends to snack all day long. Where are you taking me?"

"It's a surprise," he said with a wink, and closed the door.

Chase slid into the driver's seat and started the engine with a quick flip of his wrist. Air-conditioning blew through the vents, cooling down the hot car.

"Whew, that feels so good," Josey said with a long sigh.

The comment was innocent enough, but her soft Southern drawl made it seem otherwise. Normally he would have a comeback full of sexual innuendo, but he politely refrained.

"Am I dressed appropriately, or should we stop by my place so I can change?"

The memory of her yellow thong he had glimpsed earlier flashed through his brain. He glanced over at her dress, which tied around the neck and left her shoulders bare. With a sudden jolt of heat, he realized that she was braless. The image of her in nothing but the thong had him clenching his jaw. This was going to be a night of sheer torture.

"Chase?"

"Hmm?" He carefully kept his eyes on the road.

"You didn't answer my question."

Question? Oh, yeah. "The dress is perfect for the evening I have planned."

"Good." She removed her hat and tossed it onto the backseat. "Oh, no," she said with a giggle. "Hat head." She fluffed her hair, running her fingers through it and shaking her head at her reflection in the visor mirror.

He glanced her way to give a reassuring comment and caught her applying some silky red lip gloss. She smacked her lips together. Good God, the woman looked downright edible. Totally forgetting what he was going to say, he refocused on the road, thankful that the deli was just around the corner.

"I'll be right back," he said after parking.

Josey smiled after he got out of the car, which he had left running. He seemed jittery, almost nervous, and was working *so* hard at being a gentleman that she found it totally endearing. When he came out of the shop carrying a big picnic basket, she grinned. "Aww, how sweet," she sighed. She was going to have to sabotage his carefully laid-out plan of *not* getting laid.

After tucking the picnic basket into the trunk, he got back into the car.

"Where are you taking me?"

"To the pops concert in the park down by the river."

Josey angled her head at him, but he kept his eyes

on the road. "They're doing Broadway show tunes. My absolute favorite," she said softly. "How did you know?"

"What a coincidence." He grinned. My favorite too."

Josey giggled. "Liar." She watched him shift the gears with practiced ease, even though the traffic was heavy. The confines of the luxurious car suddenly seemed to shrink as she became more and more aware of the man sitting next to her. She had never made love in a car before, but the thought suddenly sounded appealing.

She pursed her lips while she wondered what he would do if she just nonchalantly placed her hand on his hard thigh, which flexed and bulged nicely each time he used the clutch. Her heart thudded at the thought, but before she could work up the nerve, he pulled into a parking lot.

"Here we are," he said, sounding a little strained but giving her a big smile.

Let's just go back to my place and have our picnic in bed, her brain screamed. "Oh, good. I can hear the symphony warming up."

Josey reached for her door handle but could see him hurrying around to open the door for her, so she waited. He politely offered his hand and helped her from the car. Josey swallowed. Even that brief contact had her tingling with sexual awareness.

They walked around to the rear of the car. Chase handed her the blanket while he retrieved the picnic basket. Strains of woodwinds warming up filtered through the balmy breeze while they walked across the parking lot flanked by woods on one side and the Ohio River on the other. The thick, manicured grass surrounding the amphitheater was already dotted with blankets, coolers, and lawn chairs.

"Where do you want to sit?" Josey asked.

"Off to the side if you don't mind," he said, and headed over toward the trees.

Josey's heart skipped a beat. Did he want privacy?

"I know you'd like to be closer, but if I get recognized, we'll get bugged all night for autographs," he explained with such apology in his voice that she had to smile. The irony didn't escape her that Chase had the fame and money that Cal always craved. Cal would have eaten the recognition up with a spoon.

"It's not that I mind," he continued. "I just don't want to ruin your evening." He set the basket down and helped her spread out the blanket.

Josey joined him on the blanket and kicked off her sandals. "Now, what goodies do you have in here?" she asked, and opened the wicker lid. "Oh, my!" The basket contained a feast of her favorite foods—Brie, crackers, strawberries, pâté, a bottle of merlot, and, *oh, wow,* Godiva chocolates. Oh, and no paper plates or napkins, but delicate china, real silverware, and wine goblets. "This is simply divine."

Chase smiled, looking pleased with himself. "You get to keep the basket and stuff."

"This must have cost you a fortune."

"You're worth it."

God, but she wanted him to kiss her. She swayed toward him and put a hand on his thigh.

"Hand me the wine and I'll uncork it."

It took a moment for his request to get past her desire. "Oh, okay." She handed him the bottle and corkscrew. After he deftly removed the cork with a smooth *pop,* he poured the wine into her goblet and then filled his own.

As the sun sank lower in the sky, the symphony came to life, starting with a medley of songs from *The Sound of Music.* Sipping her wine, Josey swayed to the lively beat. "This is wonderful," she told him as she spread some pâté on rice crackers. "Want one?"

He wrinkled his nose. "That's liver, right?"

Josey chuckled and took a bite. "Oh, you don't know what you're missing." She polished off the cracker and then asked, "How about a strawberry?"

"Now, that I can do."

Josey picked up a big juicy strawberry and brought it up to his mouth. When he took a bite, red juice trickled down his chin. With a low giggle, she leaned in close with a linen napkin and dabbed at his chin. Then, instead of giving him the rest, she sank her teeth into the sweet strawberry. "Oh, yumm. Would you like more?"

You know I do, he wanted to growl at her, and pin her body beneath his. "I'm fine," he lied.

"Brie?"

"I'm an American-cheese kinda guy. Maybe Colby on an adventurous day."

She smiled at him with those shiny red lips and he took a gulp of wine.

"You know you could have gotten fried chicken and potato salad and I would have been fine with that, Chase."

"I wanted to please you."

She bit into a strawberry that was the same color as her mouth and then angled her head at him. "Do you really want to please me?"

His heart thudded and he managed to nod.

She leaned forward and placed her small hand on his chest. He wondered if she could feel the wild beat of his heart.

"Well, then, I want you to—"

"Mr. Mitchell, can I have your autograph?"

Chase pushed up from his elbows and managed to smile at the youngster thrusting a scrap of paper and a pen in his direction. The interruption brought him back to his senses. He had vowed to show her there was more to him than sex, and by God, he was going to prove it. He scratched his signature on the paper and handed it to the boy with a strained smile.

"That was sweet of you," Josey said as the boy scampered away.

He shrugged. "Comes with the territory." Chase wasn't sure if he was glad for the untimely interruption or not. He chanced a glance over at her and swallowed. She was eyeing him like *he* was dessert. "By the way, where are those chocolates?" he asked with a nervous hitch in his voice.

While humming to "Seventy-six Trombones," she opened the basket and found the box. Lifting the lid, she took a piece and handed him the rest. He was contemplating which piece to choose when he heard her moan.

"Oh, this is sinful." With her head tilted to the side and her eyes shut, she let the chocolate melt in her mouth and then slowly licked the dark smear from her thumb and forefinger.

"You're not playing fair, Josey." Damn it, he wanted to show her there was more to him, and she was making it all but impossible. He wanted to shove her back onto the blanket and make wild love to her.

She opened her eyes and tried to give him an innocent look. It was comical.

"Oh, don't bat those blue eyes at me."

"What do you mean?" She frowned and he wondered if he was reading her all wrong. And then he remembered. She was a drama teacher. An actress.

"I'm doing my best to be Mr. Goody fucking Two-shoes and you're trying to turn me every way but loose. You're not playing fair!" he repeated, getting ticked.

Her driving-him-crazy red mouth rounded into a surprised "Oh" and then thinned into an angry line. "I didn't realize this was a competition." Her blue eyes stopped batting and narrowed.

He had just made a tactical error. "No . . . wait a minute. Why are you so angry?"

"You've made me feel . . . cheap."

"Cheap?"

She gave him an elegant wave of her hand. "Tacky." She began stuffing things back into the wicker basket, paused to drain the last of her wine, and then turned to him with her hands on her hips. "Take me home. Now!"

"Oh, give me a break." Okay, now *he* was pissed. Pissed because he had refrained from touching her, and now he had ruined his romantic . . . whatever the hell this date thing was. He had tried so hard to please her. "We're staying."

"Then I'm walking."

"Like hell!"

With a little lift of her chin, she got up and started across the lawn, completely forgetting her sandals.

"Forget something?" He let the straps dangle from his fingers.

She marched over to the blanket and reached for the sandals, but he held them just out of her reach. With a little squeal, she lunged for the shoes, tripped on the edge of the blanket, and fell heavily against his chest.

Ah, he finally had her just where he wanted. With a moan, Chase wrapped his arms around her. . . .

And she struggled like a wild woman. "Let go of me!" she hissed.

He tightened his hold, about to kiss her when—and he was quite sure by accident—she kneed him in the groin. White-hot pain had him gasping for air and he gladly let her go.

"Oh, God, I'm sorry." She came up to her knees and hovered over him. "Chase?"

His eyes remained shut and he clenched his jaw while breathing in short little girlie gasps.

"Chase?" she ventured again.

He waited while the pain slowly subsided to a dull throb and then opened his eyes. "I'll take you home now."

～ chapter
nine

They rode home in strained silence, angry with themselves, and at each other.

"You can keep the basket," he said as he pulled into her driveway.

"I don't want the basket," she threw back at him, and fumbled for the door handle. Finally finding it, she wrenched the door open and got out.

Chase was at a loss. Pride kept him from following her, but he wanted to make sure she entered the house safely. With her back ramrod straight, she marched up the sidewalk and unlocked her front door. He heard it slam shut and winced.

"I don't need this crap!" he muttered, and shifted into reverse. But then he spotted her yellow hat lying on the backseat and paused. *Maybe she'll need the hat,* he thought, knowing she wouldn't. *And I don't want that damned picnic basket cluttering up my car,* he reasoned. With a flick of his wrist, he killed the ignition, picked up the floppy hat and the picnic basket, and got out of the car.

Still fuming, he stomped up the sidewalk and pushed the doorbell button hard. Tapping his foot, he waited and then rang the doorbell again, longer this time. When she answered the door he was going to give her hell. Yeah, he was going to call her a . . . a spoilsport. No, make that a dick tease. Ha, that's what she was. A damned dick tease. He shifted his weight from one foot to the other.

Finally, she swung the door open. He thrust the hat forward and opened his mouth and . . . *oh, man*, she was crying.

She took the hat, crushing it in the process, and tried to shut the door, but he jammed his foot in. "Yeouch!"

She stepped back in surprise, looking *almost* sorry that she hurt him, and he limped into the house. "Josey—"

"Go away." She sniffed loudly and showed him her back.

Chase set the picnic basket down with a thump. "No. Listen, I'm sorry I got so angry, but you were teasing me and—"

She whirled around, causing the yellow skirt of her dress to whip around her legs. "I was not! A tease, Chase Mitchell, is when someone isn't planning on. . . ." She trailed off and turned bright pink.

"You mean you wanted to—"

"Yes!"

"But you said—"

"Forget what I said!"

"What kind of game are we playing here, Josey?" He took a step closer and brushed away a tear with his thumb.

She gave him a watery smile that tugged at his heart. "I'm not sure, but maybe we should set up some ground rules?"

"Such as?" he asked gruffly, and pulled her close.

She closed her eyes. "I have no idea."

"Then how about this? We take it as it comes." He was getting hard and he knew she could feel it.

She hesitated, shaking her head in denial.

"I thought you were going to give me a chance?"

Oh, boy. He hoped he played the right card.

Josey looked up at him and he hoped she could see the sincerity in his eyes. "I have issues, Chase. With men and marriage. If you were smart, you'd hit the door and keep right on walking."

He grinned. "I'm just a dumb jock."

"I'm seri—"

He cut her off with a kiss and then leaned his forehead against hers. "That damned mouth of yours has been driving me crazy all night long."

She chuckled. "I was trying."

"I know, you little tease."

"I told you, I wasn't teasing. I was seducing." Josey crooked a finger at him and then pointed at the picnic basket. "Come with me . . . and bring the basket."

He raised his eyebrows, but was more than willing to follow orders.

"I want to finish our picnic in bed."

He followed her down a short hallway, lugging the basket while admiring the gentle sway of her backside. When they entered her bedroom, she turned one small lamp on low, kicked off her sandals, and climbed onto the four-poster bed.

"Come here," she said, and patted the bedspread.

After placing the basket at the foot of the bed, Chase kicked his shoes off and joined her. Lifting the wicker lid, he found the wine.

"Let me help," she offered, and held the glasses while he removed the cork and then poured.

They sipped the wine in silence. Chase eyed her over the rim of his glass and noticed that she seemed more at ease, more confident in her own sexy skin. He knew she wanted him. Her nipples were tight and pointed through the yellow fabric. He imagined untying the knot and letting her breasts tumble free in his hands, his mouth.

But first he had questions and he wanted them answered. "Has your ex been back?"

She looked at him in surprise and set her glass down on the nightstand. "I saw him drive by once, but he didn't stop."

Chase's hand tightened on the stem of the glass. "If he's bothering you or scaring you, I'll take care of him."

She leaned over and kissed him lightly on the lips, but shook her head. "I know Cal acted like a jackass the other night, but that was totally out of character. He's usually easygoing and actually quite charming."

Chase suddenly felt like a clod in comparison. He bet Cal ate pâté. He took a big gulp of the wine and wished he had a beer instead. "Unlike big, bad me?" Her eyes rounded in surprise and Chase thought he might actually be blushing. Well, now, why did he say that?

"Let me explain something to you, Chase."

"Yeah, do," he said a little too sharply.

"My relationship with Cal Cooper started way back in college when we were cast as the leads in *Annie Get Your Gun*. We hit it off and started dating off and on, but he left for New York to act, while I just wanted to teach. Over the years, we kept running into each other, kinda like *When Harry Met Sally*."

Chase drained his wine. "And you finally fell in love?"

Josey shrugged her shoulders. "I thought so. We had so much in common, you know? Anyway, he had some mild success here and there. Eventually, he landed that part on the soap."

"You were already teaching?"

She nodded. "Had been for a while, but I always did summer theater. Lo and behold, I was trying out for *Annie Get Your Gun* and Cal came into town and . . ."

"You ended up doing the play together like in college."

She nodded. "It was a dinner theater and at the end of the run, they offered Cal the job as director. He took it and we ended up getting married."

Chase shook his head. "So what went wrong?"

"Small-town life just didn't agree with him. And I wanted children, but he was absolutely against having kids." She sighed. "He needed the excitement of the big city. When he was asked to reprise his role on *Loving Ways* he jumped at the part."

Chase frowned. "I thought they killed him off."

"It's a *soap opera*. He came back as the evil twin. Anyway, he wanted me to go with him, but I loved teaching."

"You could have taught in New York."

Josey nodded slowly. "Yes, and that's what a good wife would have done. I just don't know if this old Alabama girl could have survived the Big Apple." She shrugged and blew out a shaky sigh. "I know now that I just didn't love him enough. If you love somebody enough, you would follow them to the ends of the earth, don't you think?"

"Yeah, I suppose so. But he could have stayed, Josey. Don't blame yourself."

"I just felt like if—"

"Hey, high-profile careers are hard for any couple to deal with."

"You sound as if you know firsthand."

Chase shook his head. "No, but I sure did see it enough. Being on the road is rough, and I saw plenty of married guys screwing around and thinking nothing of it. Women wanting nothing more than to do it with someone famous—married or not, it didn't matter."

Josey leaned close and put a hand on his chest. "You might think you're all big and bad, but I think you're just a big pussycat."

Chase laughed. "Don't tell the team, okay? I've got a reputation to uphold."

"My lips are sealed."

"Oh, really?"

"Ummhmm," she said while keeping her mouth tightly closed.

With a low chuckle, Chase teased her with licks

and nibbles until she gave in with a groan, and opened her mouth for him. After a long kiss, he looked down at her and tried to keep the tone of his voice serious when he said, "I have to know something."

"What's on your mind?" she asked softly.

"Are you wearing a thong?"

Her eyes rounded in surprise and then she gave him a slow grin. "Well, now. Why don't you just find out for yourself?"

⤴ chapter
ten

Josey held her breath while he leaned forward and untied the knot at the back of her neck. The yellow fabric slid down, revealing her bare breasts, leaving her naked to the waist. With a soft moan, he cupped them in his hands, rubbing the nipples with his thumbs. Her eyes fluttered shut when his warm mouth captured one sensitive nipple, licking, sucking one and then the other.

Needing to feel his skin, Josey slid her hands underneath his shirt and over his smooth back while he continued to feast on her breasts. Wanting his warm skin against her own, she tugged at his shirt until he straightened up and pulled it over his head.

"God, you have a great chest," she said, and ran her hands over his pecs and through the silky, springy hair.

He chuckled low in his throat. "And so do you."

She pushed him back against the pillows and un-buckled his belt. His erection strained against his zip-per. With a little moan, she ran her hand over the steely hardness and unbuttoned his pants.

"Where are you going?" he asked when she rolled away and stood up.

"Don't you want to know if I'm wearing that thong?"

"Yes."

"I've never worn one before, Chase," she said as she reached back to unzip her dress. The dress fluttered to a yellow pool against the dark carpet. "I wore this for your eyes only."

"Let's keep it that way," he growled, making her shiver.

Josey would have been self-conscious, but the de-sire smoldering in his brown eyes made her bold. She stood with her head held high, her breasts thrust for-ward, and only the tiny yellow triangle of silk cover-ing her sex.

"Hey, where are you going?" he demanded hoarsely when she turned away and headed for the bathroom.

"Getting some toys," she tossed over her shoulder.

"Toys?" he said weakly. "Get back here. I'm the only toy you need."

Josey laughed as she gathered together vanilla-scented oil and candles that she used when taking a long bath. She reentered the bedroom, lit several can-dles, and doused the light.

"Now where are you going?"

"To warm the oil in the microwave and get a few

more things that I need. You get naked and pull back the covers. I'll be right back."

"You know you're killing me."

"It will be worth the wait," Josey promised as she headed for the kitchen. She warmed the oil and then found a can of whipped cream in the fridge. Her whole body tingled with anticipation. She really had no particular plan, but figured she would have fun winging it. With the hot oil in one hand and the cold can in the other, she returned to the bedroom.

"Oh, my God," he said as he eyed the whipped cream.

Josey giggled, and playfully shook the can of cream. As ordered, he had turned down the covers and was gloriously naked. She couldn't wait to rub him down. After setting the oil and cream on the nightstand, she located the picnic basket, now sitting on the floor. Bending over, she knew she was giving him quite a view as she found the box of chocolates and the strawberries.

"Would you *please* get into this bed?"

"In just one little minute," she promised as she walked across the room to her CD player and turned on some soft music. Finally ready, she turned around and walked slowly over to the bed, never taking her eyes off of him.

The flickering flame of the candles cast shadows on the wall while bathing the room with a soft glow. A vanilla scent wafted through the air, and the plaintive sound of a saxophone set a sultry mood. Josey climbed up onto the mattress, swung her leg across his waist to straddle him, and swayed with the music.

"Josey, I don't know what you're gonna do to me, but I can't last much longer."

"Oh, yes, you can." She reached behind him and fluffed up the pillows, causing her nipples to graze his chest. Then, she picked up a plump strawberry and fed it to him. "You know what's good with strawberries?"

"You?"

"Mmmm, yes . . . and chocolate." Taking a truffle from the box, she took a bite, then swirled the decadence around in her mouth before leaning down and kissing him.

The flavor of strawberry lingering in his mouth mixed with the chocolate on her tongue. Kissing him deeply, Josey let her breasts rub up and down over his chest, and her slick heat move over his hot, hard cock already sheathed in a condom.

"Josey . . . *please!*"

"Not yet," she told him, even though she pulsed with need. Reaching over, she picked up the bottle of warm oil and dribbled it over his chest. Scooting down, she began rubbing his shoulders, his chest, and then his flat stomach. Brushing lightly over his erection, she kneaded his thighs, paused to put more oil in her hands, and then continued her path until he was gleaming in the flickering light. She shimmied out of her thong and then slowly rubbed the remaining oil off of her hands and onto her own body.

"Josey, I'm hanging on by a thread."

"But I haven't used the whipped cream yet and I wanted to squirt it on your—"

"To hell with the whipped cream!" With a growl, he grabbed her around her waist, playfully flipped her over onto her back, and then plunged inside her with one sure stroke, making her cry out with pleasure. "Wrap your legs around me."

She did, and he continued thrusting hard, filling her, pounding her. The bed groaned, squeaked, the sounds mingling with those of their lovemaking. Their shadows danced on the walls while the saxophone wailed.

Josey arched up. He was so big, so powerful, but she gritted her teeth and took all of him . . . wanting more, *needing* more. He grabbed her ass cheeks and lifted her up, drawing his cock out and then pounding it back in, again and again, slapping against her. Panting hard, she dug her fingers into the bunched muscles of his shoulders and hung on while the intense pleasure spiraled upward, building, climbing. . . .

The angle of his thrusts caused just enough sweet friction against her clitoris to make her hang on the edge of an orgasm. Needing the release, she went wild beneath him until wave after wave of pleasure washed over her.

Mumbling words of love in her ear, Chase stiffened, holding her against him as he cried out, "Aahh, Josey. What have you done to me?" And then he kissed her tenderly, in sharp contrast to the wild encounter.

They collapsed against the pillows and she laid her head on his chest. He was warm and damp and slick with oil. His heart thumped wildly beneath her cheek. Coming up on one elbow, she stroked his damp curling hair off of his forehead and traced her finger over his lips.

"You are amazing, Chase Mitchell." She smoothed

a hand over his chest hair and sighed the long sigh of a very contented woman.

He chuckled. "This isn't the night I had planned. I was supposed to—"

She lightly touched a finger to his lips. "I know, I know, show me how much more there is to you than sex."

"I guess I failed miserably."

She trailed a finger over his chest and smiled. "I guess you did," she said, meaning to joke around, but he went silent with a brooding look set to his strong jaw. Now was the time to tell him how much he had come to mean to her and that the awesome sex was a by-product of the intensity of her growing feelings for him . . . but damn it, she was scared.

His chest rose and fell with a long sigh.

Oh, to hell with it, she decided, and opened her mouth to tell him that she was falling hard for him. "Chase," she began, but he interrupted.

"Oh, Josey, *don't.*"

"Don't what?"

"Give me the 'no strings attached' speech. I've heard it before."

She blinked at him.

"Well, okay, I've *given* it."

She drew in a breath. *Well.* "Is that what you think? That I'm just a forty-year-old sex-starved divorcée who wants you just to get off?" She pushed up into a sitting position and shot him a glare.

"*Is* that what you want from me, Josey?"

"You must think I'm pathetic."

"Josey . . . no, wait!" He grabbed her arm when

she would have hopped from the bed. "It's no fun to be thought of that way, is it?"

The angry fire in Josey fizzled as if doused with cold water. Suddenly, she got it. "And that's how women have treated you. Like a sex object. That's why you were so determined to show me that there's more to you, and I treated tonight as a joke. No wonder you got so angry with me." Josey felt tears well up in her throat. "God, I'm so sorry I goaded you into having sex with me. I was bound and determined to get you into my bed! God, I'm sorry!"

"I forgive you for fucking me."

"Don't call it *that*."

"Then what did we just do?" The humor was gone from his voice and he looked up at her, waiting.

"We made love," she answered softly. "There is a difference."

"Really?"

"Yes!"

"Explain it."

Flustered, embarrassed, she pulled the sheet up around her naked body, more to hide her emotions than her body. "You know what I mean."

He remained silent, avoided her gaze, and looked almost . . . hurt. With a sudden small laugh, he pulled a pillow over his head and said something that came out too muffled for her to understand.

"What did you say?" She tugged the pillow from him.

"I said I sound like such a damned *girl*." With a shake of his head, he peeked beneath the sheet. "Ah, good, it's still there."

"What?"

"My dick."

Josey laughed, partly because she knew he wanted her to, but there was still a cloud of seriousness hanging in the room. The white sheet pooled low on his waist and he still had a fine sheen of oil on his chest. Josey never thought she had much of a sex drive, but this man sent her libido into fifth gear.

"Josey, I'm sorry."

She frowned. "For what?"

"Pushing." He rolled his eyes. "Whining like I'm somehow being used and abused."

"Chase—"

He put a finger to her lips. "No, let me finish. I'm to the point in my life when I want to settle down. Up until now, my relationships with women have been mostly superficial."

Josey's heart thudded.

He cleared his throat and looked a bit uncomfortable. "But . . . I'm falling for you. Hard and fast. If you're not over your ex, or not ready to explore a serious relationship, then tell me." He stopped fiddling with the edge of the sheet and looked into her eyes.

Josey felt a stab of fear. She had the power to hurt him. He was raw sex, all hard-bodied man, but right now, even with his oiled-up muscles and dark stubble on his square jaw . . . he looked so vulnerable that it made her heart ache.

He groaned and closed his eyes. "I'm pushing again."

With the sheet still tucked up under her breasts, Josey leaned in close and brushed her lips against his mouth. His eyes opened and she gave him a trembling smile. "I'm ready."

He grinned, some of his male cockiness returning. "Hey, don't you dare tell the team that I'm a big wuss."

Josey cocked an eyebrow at him. "You're just getting in touch with your feminine side."

"Oh, stop!"

She dipped her hand beneath the sheet and found the velvety smooth, hard length of his penis, squeezing lightly, and grinned when he sucked in his breath. "What'd you say about stopping?"

"Ahh, correction. Don't."

chapter eleven

"My God, you're glowing," Erin commented as they watched the Flyers play an evening doubleheader. The stadium lights started coming to life, and the warm breeze carried the scent of popcorn and hot dogs.

Josey took a peanut Erin offered and cracked it open with the ease of an avid baseball fan. "Erin, I'm falling in love with him."

"It shows."

Josey ate the peanut and held out her hand for another. "These two weeks have been amazing. I've never felt so alive."

Erin smiled. "Love will do that to ya." She bounced up and down in her chair. "I'm so happy for you."

Josey squeezed her friend's hand. "Thank you so much for knocking some sense into me or I would have run away from the best thing that's ever happened."

"You deserve to be happy, Josey. Um, by the way, I

ran into Cal the other day at the grocery store. Did you know he's directing at the dinner theater again?"

Josey knew Erin was watching her closely for her reaction. "I haven't seen him since that awful night at my house. I really do wish him well, though."

Erin nodded. "He asked about you, and you would be proud. I was very civil to him." Her eyes suddenly got very big. "Oh!" she exclaimed, and put her hand on her tummy.

"Erin, what's wrong?"

"A kick! I felt a kick!" She grabbed Josey's hand and placed it on her rounded tummy. "Here. Feel that?"

"Oh, my God, I did!"

Peanuts forgotten, baseball forgotten, Josey spent the next few minutes feeling Erin's baby kick and move with a sense of wonder. Her eyes watered when she realized that she had always wanted children. So engrossed, they didn't realize the game was over.

"Josey!"

She looked up to see Chase leaning against the fence just past the dugout. Her heart raced at the sight of him, even though she had spent just about every waking hour with him for the past few days. With a warm smile, she hurried down the stadium steps.

"What were you doing?" he asked with a grin. "I could hear the two of you all the way into the dugout."

"The baby kicked!"

He chuckled. "Gonna be a wild one just like his daddy. Listen, I'm going to be a while getting ready for this road trip on Tuesday. Why don't you let Erin drop you off over at Shakey's and I'll be over in a little while? We'll order some burgers or wings or whatever sounds good."

Josey leaned close and whispered in his ear, "*You* sound good."

He groaned. "You're not going to make this road trip easy for me, baby."

Josey gave him a pout. "Don't mention that road trip." Bending over the railing, she gave him a quick kiss. "I'll meet you over there."

Chase arrived at the local bar and grill an hour later, desperate for a cold beer in his hand, and Josey in his arms. Weaving his way through the crowd, he paused to politely sign an autograph, chat with the grizzly old owner, and shake several hands. Someone thrust a cold longneck at him and he tipped it up in appreciation before taking a long guzzle. Finally, he arrived at what he had come to think of as "their booth" and slid in beside Josey.

She looked up with a smile that stole his breath. "I ordered some wings," she said, and pushed a basket his way. "Hot, just the way you like them."

It pleased him that she was learning his favorite things. Reaching underneath the table to squeeze her thigh, he whispered in her ear, "You're hot, just the way I like *you*."

"Stop that," she said, playfully slapping at his hand. "I'm hungry."

"Me too," he said, and nuzzled her neck. "For you."

"Chase," she giggled, and gave him a nudge with her elbow. "The waiter is here."

"Oh." He reluctantly straightened up. "Josey, what do you want? More wings?"

She wrinkled her nose.

"Hmm, how about the sampler platter and we'll share?"

She nodded. "Sounds good."

They settled into easy conversation, discussing a little bit of everything, and a whole lot about baseball.

"You should have pulled Reese Taylor sooner. He didn't have his head in the game today."

"Exactly. That's why I left him in there. That kid's gotta learn to focus. All that talent and he's a head case."

Josey took a sip of wine and then nodded. "I see your point. It's not all about winning, but teaching the game."

At that moment, Chase knew he loved her. Not only did he get hard every time he was in the same room with her, but he just simply liked *being* with her. He had waited a long time to find the right woman, but by God, it was worth the wait.

The food came, but Chase couldn't keep his hands off of her. Knowing that he was leaving for a seven-day road trip made him even more anxious to eat and get her into bed.

And tonight, he was going to tell her something he had never told a woman before . . . well, and *meant* it. He was going to tell Josey Cooper that he loved her.

"Let's get out of here," Chase said, and drained his beer.

"But we've barely touched the food."

He scanned the room for their waiter. "We'll get a

doggie bag. I enjoyed the last picnic we had in bed, and this time I get to have bar food instead of that sissy stuff."

Josey wiggled her eyebrows. "I still have the whipped cream." Leaning close, she whispered in his ear just where she was going to squirt it and lick it off.

Chase moaned. "If I get a speeding ticket, it's all your fault. Just remember that."

Josey giggled, but turned in surprise when she heard her name called. Her eyes widened when she saw Cal approach their booth. Feeling a little uncomfortable, she took a deep breath, realizing she was going to have to get used to the idea that he was back in Sander's City. "Hello, Cal," she said with a little lift of her chin.

Cal smiled at her and gave Chase a brief nod. "I hate to interrupt," he said, and actually looked a little nervous, "but I need your help."

"My help?" Josey's hand was on Chase's thigh. She could feel the muscles tense beneath the soft denim, so she smiled, wanting to keep things friendly.

"Yes, I'm doing a production of *The Sound of Music* this fall and I'm searching for some local talent. Since you're the drama teacher at Sander's High, I thought you might know some kids who could play the von Trapp children."

"Oh . . . why, sure. I had heard you had taken the director's job at the dinner theater. Hmm, I can think of a few already." Josey smiled and Cal seemed to relax. "Wow, *The Sound of Music?* That's quite an undertaking."

"And one of your favorites, as I recall." He angled his head and gave her a patented Cal Cooper smile. "You wouldn't be interested in trying out for the part of Maria, would you?"

Josey laughed. "I'm afraid I'm a bit too old for Maria. The mother superior would be more like it." Josey would have continued the conversation, but Chase had become very still and quiet. She glanced up at him, but his face was an impassive mask. She cleared her throat nervously and turned her attention back to Cal.

"I'll give you my card," he offered, and reached into his pocket for his wallet. "It has all of my contact info on it."

Josey nodded as she accepted the card and tucked it into her purse. "I'll get the names of the students to you, Cal. Good luck. Um, Chase and I were leaving," she said, glancing up at him. "Weren't we?"

"Yeah."

"Oh," Cal said, his gaze lingering on Josey and then glancing at Chase as if he wanted to say something. "Listen," he began, but Chase interrupted.

"Josey, are we leaving or not?" His voice was low and smooth, but held a hint of something she didn't like.

"Yes," she said as she slid from the booth. "Good night, Cal." Not sure whether to shake his hand or hug him, she simply gave him a small smile and turned to Chase, who was busy paying the bill.

He turned to her after tossing a tip onto the table.

"Don't you want that doggie bag?" Josey asked

with a bright smile, knowing he was upset. She would have been flattered by jealousy, but she instinctively knew it went further than that. His dark eyes were stormy.

"I'm not hungry," he said, and headed for the door.

chapter twelve

Josey hurried to keep up with Chase's long, angry strides across the gravel parking lot. Although the night was warm, sultry, Josey shivered. She followed Chase to the car, where he opened her door in stony silence. Surely he didn't think there was anything going on between her and Cal, did he?

Josey fiddled with the straps of her purse while trying to think of the best way to approach the subject. When they stopped for a red light, she decided to just dive right in. "Talk to me, Chase," she pleaded. "Come on, surely you don't think there is something between me and Cal, do you?"

He didn't respond, but the white-knuckled grip he had on the gearshift shouted his answer. Finally, he angled his head in her direction. "Why didn't you tell me he was moving back to Sander's City?"

Josey swallowed. "I just found out, myself, from Erin—"

"And when were you going to tell me? Or were you? Damn it, I thought you were over him." The light turned green and he stepped on the gas pedal a little too hard, throwing Josey back against the soft leather.

"Slow down!" she pleaded, gripping the armrest. She suddenly recalled his earlier comment about breaking the speed limit and almost burst into tears.

And then she got pissed.

The reasonable part of her brain screamed to explain to him that she was over Cal, and that he wasn't a threat to what they had. The other part wanted to scream at him to quit being so damned stupid!

The reasonable part of her brain would have beaten the pissed-off side if he hadn't been going so fucking fast. Gritting her teeth, she refused to ask him again to slow down, even though the black Beemer could probably go a million miles an hour. Tires squealed around a hairpin turn, sending her heart into her throat. She instinctively pressed her right foot on the nonexistent brake on her side and held her breath.

Sirens and blue lights brought the joyride to an end.

Cursing under his breath, Chase shot her a glare.

"Don't you dare blame this on me!" she hissed as the officer approached.

Oh, but Chase was smooth and it didn't hurt that the officer recognized him, finally letting him off with a friendly—*yes, friendly!*—warning. That angered her even more.

"He would have given me a ticket," she grumbled.

"Yeah, right. You would have batted your baby blues and he would have let you off."

"I would never have used my femininity to get me out of a punishment I deserved!" she said with a haughty lift of her chin, knowing full well she was lying.

He snorted.

"Pull over."

"What?"

"You heard me. I'm getting out."

"No. It's not safe and we're at least two miles away from your house."

"Pull the damned car over!"

He didn't, but at the stop sign, she reached for the handle. He was too quick, and pushed the button that wouldn't let her unlock the door.

He gave her a smug, tight little smile. "Child safety feature."

Josey had never been quick to anger, but right now, she thought she might explode. "You . . ." She searched her brain for a name vile enough and drew a blank. There wasn't one. "Jerk!" she sputtered.

He snorted again, and she decided that snorting was her least favorite sound in the world. Tears pricked at the back of her eyelids, but she *refused* to let them fall. She swallowed hot moisture and breathed a ragged sigh of relief when he turned down her street. He pulled up to the curb with a jerky halt.

"Unlock the damned door before I damage your fancy car."

He sighed and ran a hand over his face. "You know, Josey, all I wanted was honesty. Did you know all along Cal was moving back here?"

Josey was so shocked, she could only blink at him.

He must have taken her silence as a yes, but before she could deny his ridiculous accusation, he kept on going.

"You know, if you had told me you were looking for a hot little summer fling to piss off your ex, I would have understood. I told you, I'm playing for keeps, so go ahead—have an affair with one of those young stud ballplayers. Reese Taylor is a prime candidate. I'll put in a good word for you."

Josey gasped and could only gape at him in the dim light of the car. But then anger dissolved into despair, leaving her body feeling heavy against the cushy leather seat. With effort, she turned to him. "Unlock the door," she said tiredly.

He looked at her for a long moment and Josey could sense the hurt he was feeling as well. And while a part of her wanted to put her arms around him and tell him how wrong he was about her . . . she just couldn't. She shouldn't have to. If he thought she had lied to him and wanted him only for a hot summer fling, well, then, they were over.

When he pushed the unlock button, the click seemed loud and final. Josey fumbled for the handle and opened the door. As she swung her legs out to the curb, he called her name, but she kept on going.

If he came after her, pulled her into his strong embrace, she would be helpless to resist, but she heard his engine rev up and the squeal of tires on pavement.

Feeling as heavy as lead, her legs somehow made it up the sidewalk and she searched for her keys through the blur of tears. Finally, she gave up and slumped down to the front stoop. Cradling her head in her hands, she cried for the five years of a wasted marriage, for the babies she never had, for the dreams that were broken.

But most of all, she cried for the loss of Chase Mitchell and what could have been.

After a while—minutes, hours?—she pulled herself to her feet, found her keys, and stumbled into her house. Feeling horribly empty, she went through the motions of getting ready for bed.

Sleep, of course, wouldn't come. "Oh, damn, damn . . . *damn!*" she shouted to the silent, empty room. Punching the pillow, she tossed and turned, cursed, and finally cried until she fell into an exhausted, dreamless sleep.

❦ chapter
thirteen

Josey woke up the next morning feeling like it was the day after a margarita night. Her head throbbed; her body ached. She felt completely drained. With a groan, she rubbed her gritty eyes and managed to stumble from her bed to the bathroom. Extreme bed head and red-rimmed, puffy eyes faced her in the mirror.

"Yikes! I look like something the cat dragged in." Blinking at her reflection, she decided that the cat wouldn't have bothered. She rolled her head around on her shoulders and yawned. "Coffee. I need coffee."

While her coffee gurgled and hissed into the pot, she plopped down onto her sofa and watched the morning news while making a list of things to do. She knew that keeping busy was the key to getting over Chase, so she made the list a long one.

Josey needed a sympathetic shoulder. She thought about calling Erin but didn't want to upset her. Her mother was still in denial over her divorce, so calling her wasn't an option either. Most of her old college friends were soccer moms driving SUVs, and although she was friendly with a handful of twenty-something teachers over at Sander's High, she didn't feel close enough to any of them to confide in them. Josey sighed, feeling self-pity and loneliness crashing down on her.

She slammed her fist onto the table hard enough to make the salt and pepper shakers go airborne. "I'm through with self-pity," she muttered, tossing her pen onto the table. With a determined lift of her chin that trembled only a little, she pushed back from the table and poured steaming coffee into a huge mug and added a splash of cream.

Fortified with three mugs of coffee and a bowl of Froot Loops, Josey headed to the bathroom, where she brushed her teeth and pulled her hair back into a stubby ponytail. Dressed in old stretchy workout shorts and a shabby T-shirt, she began knocking off the mighty tasks on her list.

By midmornng she was sweaty, tired, and in the mother of all foul moods. She realized why she avoided things like cleaning out the refrigerator and dusting the miniblinds: She hated it! Not only were these tasks hard and boring, but also more importantly, all of her sweat-producing elbow grease was *not* keeping her mind off of Chase.

Every damn thing reminded her of him. The leftovers she tossed from the fridge were from dinners shared with him. The music on the radio reminded her of him.

"Damn you, Chase Mitchell!" she shouted, and threw her sponge to the tile floor with a wet splat.

With a stomp of her foot, she glanced down at the list on the kitchen table. "Oh, joy. Now I get to clean out the pantry."

She was in the middle of tossing canned goods purchased in the Middle Ages when the phone rang. Her heart pounded. What if it was *him*? Not wanting to appear too eager, she let it ring three times before picking up.

"Hello?" She tried to cover up her breathless voice.

"Hey, Josey, it's Erin."

Josey slumped into a kitchen chair. "Oh, hi."

"Listen," Erin said, sounding way too cheerful, "Michael and I are thinking of driving up to Akron to watch the Flyers play. You wanna come?"

Josey wrinkled her nose as she tossed a can of cream-of-celery soup into the trash. "No, thanks. I'm really busy."

"Doing what?"

"Stuff."

"What kind of stuff?" Erin asked, and Josey could hear the frown in her voice.

She blew the dust off of a can of tuna. "Important stuff."

"More important than surprising Chase by showing up to cheer the Flyers on?"

"He'd be surprised all right," Josey muttered.

"Oh, my God, you broke up!"

"Yep."

"But why? The two of you seemed so perfect together."

Josey swallowed, trying to keep her voice level. "He thinks I only want him for sex."

"Isn't that supposed to be your line?"

Josey laughed without much humor.

"Why in the world would he think that?"

Josey sighed. "Cal showed up at Shakey's, and Chase thinks there's still something between us. God, Erin, he thinks I just want him to make Cal jealous or something. . . . I don't know."

"That's absurd."

She felt her throat tighten up. "Tell me about it."

"Didn't you set him straight?"

"I tried, Erin. But you know, if that's all he thinks of me, well, then, I'm better off without him."

"You don't really believe that. I've never seen you so happy. Come on, go with us tonight."

"No," she answered quietly. "I'm all through with pain and heartache."

Erin sighed on the other end of the line. "I won't push, but I think you're making a big mistake. I understand how his accusation hurt, but if you really love him, then you should fight for his love."

"I shouldn't have to defend myself! He believed the worst of me."

"No, you shouldn't. But love makes people think crazy things, *do* crazy things. You're miserable and I'm sure he is too. He probably regrets his actions already. I just bet you'll get a dozen red roses before the day is done."

Josey leaned back in her chair. "Erin, don't you *dare* interfere! Promise me!"

"Okay, I promise! If you change your mind and decide to go, just call."

"Okay."

Josey hung up the phone and continued cleaning out her pantry. Indecision hung over her head like a dark cloud right next to her angry cloud of depression as she purged her house of all unwanted, outdated, or never used items. Was her pride getting in the way? Should she go to the game? Yes! Yes, she should!

Josey ran from the mountain of junk in her garage, back into the kitchen, and picked up the phone. "No!" She slammed the phone back into the cradle. She argued with herself like an insane person, picking up the phone and slamming it down several times until the sound of the doorbell made her pause in mid-slam. She placed the phone in the cradle, gently this time, and hurried to the front door.

A young man stood on her small porch holding a bouquet of, not red, but yellow roses. "Are you Josey Cooper?"

"Yes."

He smiled. "Well, then, these are for you."

With a pounding heart, Josey opened the door. "Thank you," she said as she took the big glass vase from him with a shaky smile. On unsteady legs, she walked into the kitchen and placed the vase on the oak table. After chewing on her lip for a long moment, she removed the card and opened the envelope and immediately recognized the large, flowing handwriting.

"*Dear Josey,*" she softly read out loud.

> *I've learned in the past year that the old saying "You don't know what you've got 'til it's gone" is true. You've probably guessed*

by now that one of the reasons I'm back in Sander's City is you.

Josey put a hand to her mouth and felt a tear trickle down her face. Taking a deep breath, she read the rest of the note.

But after seeing you with Chase Mitchell, and seeing the way you looked at each other, I know that there is no hope for me. I realize now that we were better friends than lovers, but I want you to know that I will always love you. Take this second chance, Josey. You deserve everything that I was too busy to give you.

Josey read the note three times and finally felt a sense of closure. With a trembling smile, she leaned in and inhaled the delicate scent of the roses and let her cheek brush against the velvety petals. How ironic that flowers from her ex-husband had her reaching for the phone once again, and this time she wasn't going to hang up.

When Erin answered, Josey asked, "Is your offer still open to go to Akron?"

"Sure, but we're leaving soon."

"I'll be ready," Josey assured her. "Now, I only hope my plan works."

chapter fourteen

Chase was in a foul mood. He rode back to the motel in the front seat of the chartered team bus, talking to no one. Not only had the Flyers gotten their asses pounded, but he had also managed to get thrown out of the game after hotly contesting a third-strike call.

But that wasn't what really had him pissed. He was so angry with *himself* that if it were possible, he would kick his own ass. Because deep in his heart, he knew that he had misjudged Josey. He had let his own insecurities and jealousy cloud his feelings and shed doubt on something so good, so real, and he'd managed to hurt her in the process. "Male pride," he mumbled under his breath.

The bus pulled into the parking lot of the motel and wheezed to a stop. "See ya, Hank," he told the driver as he stepped off the bus. While lugging his duffel bag over to his room, he rehearsed the speech he planned to give to Josey if she would ever pick up her phone. He had tried several times during the day to reach her, and planned to try again as soon as he entered his room.

"Well, hell," he growled when he failed to find his key card in his duffel bag. "Where could it be?" He was about to hike over to the front desk when he noticed dim light shining through a crack in the drawn curtains. Leaning close to the window, he tried to see into the room. The fine hairs on his neck stood at attention when he thought he detected shadowy movement near the bed.

Was someone trying to rob him? With a pounding heart, he realized that the shadowy figure was coming toward the door. Chase took a step back, thinking that the robber *wasn't* going to get past him. Bracing his feet on the pavement, he cocked his fists and waited.

A moment later the door swung open. "Oh, my God." His jaw dropped and his fists fell to his sides.

Josey stood in the doorway wearing a baby blue high-cut teddy and a come-hither smile. She crooked a pink-tipped finger at him and he would have followed her anywhere. He absently picked up his duffel bag and entered the room, still unable to formulate words.

He closed the door with a soft click without taking his eyes off of her. His bag slipped from his fingers, landing on the carpet with a thud.

She gave him a shy smile. "Well, don't just stand there with your mouth hanging open, Chase Mitchell. Get over here and kiss me."

He was on her in two steps, dragging her into his arms. He crushed his mouth to hers and gave her a hot, hungry kiss. When she moaned, he lifted her up and she wrapped her arms and bare legs around him. The kiss went on and on. Chase kneaded the smooth skin of her nearly bare bottom while she tangled her fingers in his hair.

Still kissing her, he backed up to the edge of the bed and sat down with her straddling his lap. His erection strained against his zipper and while he hated to end the kiss, he needed to shed his clothing and plunge inside her.

"Chase," she began when the kiss finally ended. "I want you to know that—"

"No, stop," he said, gently grasping her chin. "I'm sorry for the things I said. I should never have doubted you." He rubbed his thumb over her bottom lip, shiny and swollen from his hungry mouth. "I was just scared."

"Of what?"

"Of loving you so damned much and you not loving me back." He rolled his eyes. "Aw, that wasn't very pretty. I had this whole speech planned."

"Sometimes showing is better than telling." She began unbuttoning his shirt. "Let me show you how much I love you, Chase."

He grinned. "Show-and-tell. I like this game."

"Just so you know that I'm playing for keeps."

"I love you, Josey."

Hot moisture in her throat made it difficult to respond. She swallowed and then said, "I love you too, Chase." A moment of silence passed.

"Now that we've got the telling out of the way, let's move on to the showing."

"Okay." She scooted from his lap and stood up. Very slowly, she slipped one thin strap over her shoulder, then the other. The silky material slid to her waist, baring her breasts. "Your turn."

In one swift move, he tugged his shirt over his head and tossed it to the floor.

She shimmied out of her teddy and stood before him. "Come closer," he said.

When she took a step forward, he grapped her to him. Her belly quivered when he ran his tongue in a straight line from her navel to the delicate triangle of curls. He nuzzled her there, sliding his hands from her waist to her bottom, drawing her closer. He flicked his tongue over her clit, loving her taste, her scent.

She grabbed his shoulders, leaning heavily on him for support. "Chase!"

Her husky plea had him burying his face in her nest of soft curls. He made love to her with his mouth until she cried out and collapsed against him. Gently, he rolled her over onto the bed and then shed his jeans.

"Please tell me you have a condom."

Still a little dazed from the intense orgasm, Josey blinked up at him and anticipated his next question. "Condoms are on the nightstand," she said with a shaky grin.

He gave a low whistle when he saw the small pile of packets. "You came prepared."

Josey felt the heat of a blush. "I was a woman on a mission."

After rolling on a condom, Chase joined her on the bed. "Mission accomplished," he said before giving her a long lusty kiss.

He made love to her slow and easy, bringing her closer and closer to an orgasm with each long, sure stroke of his penis. She moved her hips to the sensual rhythm . . . slowly in . . . slowly out. The muscles in his shoulders bunched and quivered beneath her hands.

Skin to skin, heart to heart, he continued to fill her, love her. She skimmed her hands over his back while arching up in an effort to get even closer. Entwining her legs with his, she rocked with him and slowly . . . *oh so slowly* her orgasm began to build.

And still he prolonged the moment, easing in and out . . . teasing, tempting, making her climb higher and higher. "Chase . . ."

"You feel so good, so hot, so sweet," he said gruffly in her ear. "I want to make love to you forever."

The heat of his words sent her flying.

He thrust hard and deep, groaning into her ear, and she shattered into a zillion pieces.

He rolled over, taking her with him. Her cheek rested against his damp chest, beating heart. She snuggled against him, feeling the contentment of a woman well loved.

"How did you get into my room?" he asked after his heart rate returned to near normal.

"Michael and Erin brought me to the game. Michael snuck into the locker room and stole your room key."

Chase chuckled. "Remind me to thank him. I hope they're not waiting to take you home, because I want you to stay with me."

"I'm not going anywhere."

He wrapped his arms around her and kissed the top of her head. "Josey?"

"Hmmm?"

"I'm not one to beat around the bush."

She gave him a throaty laugh. "I won't touch that line," she said, but her heart picked up speed.

His arms tightened around her. "I want to marry you."

She pushed back so she could look up into his eyes. "Well, then ask me."

"Josey," he began, but had to clear his throat. "Will you marry me?"

She put her hands on his cheeks, trying to smile, but her lips trembled. "I would be honored to be your wife, Chase Mitchell," she managed, and then kissed him softly.

"I'm an all-American kinda guy, Josey. You'll find me easy to please."

"Oh, and I do aim to please."

Chase gently eased her back against the pillows. "I need three simple things and you'll keep me happy."

She raised one elegant eyebrow. "And they are?"

"A steady diet of baseball, hot apple pie, and Southern-fried Josey Cooper."

Josey laughed low in her throat, and her hands reached up to graze over his chest. "You *know* I love baseball. My granny taught me how to bake an apple pie that will make you sob with pleasure. And I do believe you will find Southern-fried Josey Cooper . . . *finger lickin' good.*"

"Oh, really?" With a wicked grin, he eased his hand up her thigh, making her gasp. "I think I'll just have to find out for myself."

hotshot

~ chapter
one

"Here's to your last night out as a single woman," Halley Forrester said, raising her fluted glass of champagne in honor of her best friend, Cathy Porter, soon to be Cathy Spencer. The two other women in the bachelorette party leaned in close and clinked their glasses together.

"At least I'm doing it in style," Cathy commented, and took a sip of her champagne. "I can't believe you guys sprung for a limo. This is awesome!"

Halley gave a dismissive wave of her hand. "We got a good deal. My brother had some connections."

"I'd sure like to connect with Cole Forrester," Jenna, another bridesmaid, commented as she fanned her face with her hand. "A *love* connection."

Halley snorted. "No, you wouldn't. He goes through women like I go through panty hose. I love my brother, but I wouldn't wish him on any woman, especially one of my friends."

"Oh, I'd faint if he so much as looked at me," Jenna said with a long sigh.

Halley rolled her blue eyes. "Give me a break."

"Hasn't a guy ever made you go weak in the knees?"

The dreamy tone of Jenna's voice made Halley wrinkle her nose. "That only happens in romance novels. There's not a guy on this earth who could make me swoon." Halley shook her head at Jenna but had to grin. Although they were opposites in many ways, they had been friends since kindergarten and now both taught school over at Sander's High. In fact, all four of the women had grown up together in the quaint town overlooking the banks of the Ohio River.

Jenna tipped her strawberry blond head to the side and angled her glass at Halley. "Your day will come. And I say the tougher they are, the harder they fall."

Halley took a sip of her champagne. "Yeah, yeah, yeah. You better be watching out your window, because pigs will be flying." She turned to Cathy. "Did Rob make you weak in the knees?"

Cathy pursed her lips and then slowly shook her head. "Hmmm. No, but he sure gave me butterflies in my stomach."

"Oh, puh-lease." Halley barely refrained from rolling her eyes again. She loved these girls, but sometimes they drove her crazy. Jenna taught art, and Cathy taught English literature. Both of them had their head in the clouds, while *she* was perfectly grounded. There was nothing remotely romantic about the physical education and health that she taught. Halley turned to Sallie Adams, who owned a secondhand-clothing shop. "Sallie, help me out here."

Sallie smoothed a hand over her vintage jean skirt. "I stutter."

"What?" Halley frowned while the other women nodded in understanding.

Sallie tucked a long strand of straight black hair behind her ear and gave Halley a sheepish grin. "If a guy really turns me on, I get all tongue-tied."

Halley leaned back against the cool leather seat and shook her head. "You guys are pathetic."

Cathy clucked her tongue while she patted her gently on the leg. "You are *so* going to melt when the right guy comes along. I just hope I'm there to see it."

Jenna nodded. "I'd buy tickets to see Halley Forrester melt into a puddle at some guy's feet."

Halley sighed. Thankfully, the conversation about her love life, or lack thereof, ended when they turned down Main Street. A limo in Sander's City was not a common occurrence. Although the shops and businesses had already closed, the warm June evening had residents out and about, pushing strollers, and walking dogs. Many of them stopped at the sight of the white stretch limo, waving and elbowing their partners.

"They think someone famous is in here," Cathy said with a giggle.

"They probably think it's one of the Flyers being sent up to the majors," Halley commented. "Let's not burst their bubble by letting on it's just a bachelorette party." She held up the champagne bottle and topped off their glasses.

"Speaking of the Flyers, they had a baseball game

tonight. Shakey's will be packed when the game lets out," warned Jenna.

"I reserved a table," Halley assured them.

"I thought they didn't take reservations," said Sallie.

Halley shrugged her shoulders. "Cole knows the owner." She turned to Jenna and wiggled her eyebrows. "He said he might stop by after the baseball game."

Jenna sputtered in midswallow of champagne. "Don't you dare tell him what I said about the love connection thing."

"I won't," Halley promised, struggling to keep a straight face.

"You told him I liked him when we were in the third grade."

"You've had a thing for Cole since third grade?" asked Sallie.

Halley answered for her. "That's why the slumber parties were always at my house. She wanted to catch Cole in his Batman underwear."

"Guilty," Jenna said in a small voice.

Sallie drained her champagne and set the glass down in the drink holder with a clink. "Well, then, here's what we do."

"Don't even—" Jenna began, but Sallie held up a silencing hand.

"In honor of Cathy finding the man of her dreams, we are *all* going to find our fantasy man tonight, and get a kiss." Sallie pointed at Jenna. "You get Cole to kiss you, and you can have anything you want in my shop for half price."

Halley had to laugh. "Find our fantasy at Shakey's? It might be the hottest spot in Sander's City, but hardly the place to find our fantasy man."

"Alcohol will be clouding our judgment," Sallie reminded them. "When we have our beer goggles on, half the guys in the bar will be looking pretty hot." She leaned forward from the side bench seat and wiggled her eyebrows. "Come on, girls, tell me what turns you on."

Halley was about to tell them she wasn't going to be a part of this silly game, but Cathy clasped her hands together and said, "Oh, this is so fun. My bachelorette party is going to be a night to remember!"

"Well, girls," Sallie began, "*my* fantasy is a blond, muscle-bound hunk. You know, a guy who could bench-press me with one hand on my ass."

"And you think you'll find him at Shakey's?" Halley asked dryly. She was glad the window to the limo driver was closed.

Sallie shrugged, making her ample cleavage jiggle above her hot pink V-necked blouse. "I'll scope out the most cut guy in the place and get the rest of you to approve before I go after the kiss."

Halley groaned inwardly. This was beginning to feel like a bad episode of *Sex and the City*.

"Okay," Sallie continued, "that takes care of Jenna and me. Halley, what about you? Tell us about your fantasy man."

Halley squirmed on the smooth leather seat. She chewed on her inner lip for a moment, trying to think of someone she was least likely to find in Shakey's, thus playing the game and yet getting off of the hook. "A black guy."

"Ooooh," the group said collectively.

Halley grinned. The black population in Sander's City was slim, and she wasn't exactly lying. There, she thought smugly. She was in, and yet she wasn't.

"What about me?" asked Cathy with a pout.

"You're engaged," Halley protested as the limo pulled into the parking lot of Shakey's. "You can't play."

"Well, give me something outrageous to do. I want to earn my fifty percent off at Sallie's shop too."

"Let's *each* give her something to do," Jenna said with a giggle.

"Okay," the usually conservative Cathy said with a brave lift of her chin. "Fire away."

Jenna went first. "You've got to pinch the butt of the guy of my choice."

"No problem," Cathy told her.

Halley gave her request next. "I want you to dance like a slut to the disco song of my choice. I'm thinking 'Brick House' might be a good one."

"I can shake my booty with the best of them."

All eyes turned to Sallie, the women knowing her request would indeed be outrageous. "You've got to ask some guy for a condom and then bring it to me. And we have to see you do it. No cheating."

Cathy's chin remained raised, but her brown eyes rounded. "You *will* have your condom."

"Good," Sallie said, and polished off her drink. "I just hope I get to use it."

They giggled like teenagers while the limo driver

came around to open the door. They climbed out, getting some stares from people entering Shakey's.

"Call me on my cell when you ladies are ready to leave," the driver said with a tip of his cap.

"It'll be late," Cathy said with a laugh. "'Cause we're going to make it a night to remember."

∽ chapter two

"Oh, my God, they're little penises." Cathy snickered as she lifted the earrings from the box. The friends were sitting in a booth while Cathy opened her tasteless gag gifts.

Sallie rolled her eyes. "Call them dicks. Tonight we're naughty, remember?"

"D—" Cathy began, but put her hand over her mouth and laughed. "I c-can't."

"Jenna?" asked Sallie. "Can you say *dick*?"

"D-di . . . ," she giggled, "dick!"

"Dick, dick, *dick*," Halley chanted before being asked. "Cathy, how are you going to ask for a condom when you can't even say *dick*?"

"We need to loosen this bachelorette up," declared Sallie.

"And get her talking dirty before she's all married and proper," Jenna chimed in.

Sallie pointed at Cathy. "We're going to loosen up

with a round of shots, and you're going to order them in a loud, clear voice."

Cathy nodded, making the pink dicks now dangling from her earlobes swing back and forth. "No problem."

Sallie grinned. "I want you to order four *screaming orgasms*."

Cathy's eyes grew big when Sallie motioned for the waiter. "It's a guy!" she protested.

"You can do it," Halley whispered in her ear. "Go ahead."

The twenty-something waiter gave the women a smile. "What can I get you ladies tonight?"

"We'll have"—Cathy's lips twitched and she swallowed before trying to continue—"four. . . ."

Halley gave her a nudge with her elbow.

"Loud and clear," Sallie warned.

Cathy blinked up at the waiter and held on to the edge of the wooden table. He waited with a frown for her to continue. "We'll have four s-screaming . . . *orgasms*!" Cathy smiled proudly at successfully completing her order while blushing furiously.

"My pleasure, ladies. Coming right up."

When he left, they all dissolved into a fit of giggles. Even Sallie couldn't maintain her composure.

"I've never had a screaming orgasm," Jenna managed between giggles.

"I have," said Sallie.

"The drink, I mean," Jenna clarified.

Sallie grinned. "Oh, then me neither. How about you, Halley?"

Halley was laughing so hard, she couldn't answer.

The bar, although fairly large, with a dance floor and a stage for a live band, was filling up with the crowd from the Flyers game. While they waited for their screaming orgasms, Cathy opened her next gift, a pair of edible underwear.

The waiter arrived and served the drinks with a flourish. "Enjoy, ladies. I'm guessing this is a bachelorette party?"

"What gave us away?" Cathy asked as she warily eyed her drink.

"The dicks dangling from your ears."

Cathy blushed again and reached for her drink. She took a sniff. "What's in this?"

The waiter shrugged, and said with a grin, "If I tell you, I'll have to shoot you."

Sallie waved her hand as she picked up her shot glass. "Ladies, drink up!"

Halley tossed down her shot, feeling the warmth all the way to her toes. She watched Cathy choke hers down with a grimace. Jenna managed as well, but not without a hiss at the end. For three schoolteachers and a small-business owner, they were, by their own small-town standards, getting *pretty wild*.

The band started warming up, mixing the sound of music with the buzz of the growing Friday night crowd. Peanut shells littered the wood-planked floor, and the smell of hot wings, a Shakey's specialty, hung in the air. The women ordered a basket of wings and seasoned French fries, but opted for light beer instead of another round of shots. They might be trying to party, but by any standards, they were lightweights when it came to drinking.

"Yeow, these wings are hot," Halley commented as she reached for her beer.

"Hey, let's dance," urged Cathy when an old-school disco tune started up.

"You guys go ahead," Halley replied. "I need these wings to settle." She wiped the hot sauce from her fingers with a lemon-scented wet napkin and watched her friends bop around on the dance floor. Sallie leaned over and said something to Cathy, who laughed and started grinding her hips. Jenna poked a finger in her direction and then pointed to Cathy, who was trying her best to dance but ended up looking pretty much like Elaine on *Seinfeld*. Halley hoped they had forgotten about the game they were going to play, but figured she wasn't going to get much action in the fantasy man contest, anyway.

And then she saw him.

He stood out, not so much because he was black, but because he was gorgeous. Tall, with the build of an athlete, he walked up to the bar directly across the room from their table. When he leaned forward to grab a beer, his tan khakis molded to a butt that had her biting her bottom lip. He turned and rested an elbow against the edge of the bar, casually surveying the room. A charcoal gray shirt stretched across wide shoulders and when he tipped his beer bottle up, a muscle flexed in his biceps.

A warm feeling zinged through Halley, much like the shot she had earlier. She was wondering what it *would* be like to have his mouth covering hers, when he looked her way. Oh, God. She averted her gaze and tipped up her beer glass, hoping he didn't see her ogling him.

Halley took a quick sip of her beer and turned her attention back to the dance floor, but her thoughts remained with her fantasy man. When the girls stayed on the floor for another song, she angled her head slightly toward the bar so she could watch him without being too obvious. The bartender seemed to know him. Several people approached him and either shook his hand or gave him a high five.

And then it dawned on her. He was a Flyers ballplayer. Drumming her finger on the table, she thought for a moment, trying to recall his name. Halley had been to a few of the games at the minor-league stadium that opened last summer. The principal of her school, Erin Manning, was a huge fan, and had taken her to a few games. Halley frowned, thinking, and then she remembered. He was a pitcher . . . a good one, who had a shot at the majors. She also remembered there had been some sort of controversy surrounding him, but couldn't recall his name.

Her friends returned to the table, flushed and laughing.

"I did my slutty dance," Cathy announced. "Now it's someone's turn to kiss their fantasy man."

Halley's heart hammered in her chest while she hoped her friends didn't spot her ballplayer at the bar. For the most part, she was nervy. She was an athlete, and a competitive spirit remained part of her nature, but guys and dating had always thrown her for a loop. Losing her mother to cancer at the age of ten hadn't helped. While she loved her father and brother, Cole, dearly, they had no idea how to raise a girl.

Halley looked at her friends with envy. Sallie, the

sexpot, used her feminine wiles with practiced ease. Generous curves and long black hair helped, but it was an aura of sexiness that attracted lingering male looks in her direction. Quiet Cathy captured Rob with her sweet nature and subdued yet pretty features. Perky and petite, with innocent blue eyes, strawberry blond hair, and a smattering of freckles across her nose, Jenna brought out the protective nature in men.

Halley glanced toward the bar and wished *she* were more comfortable with her feminine allure. While she knew her toned and trim body drew male interest, and her face was pretty, she just didn't know how to be . . . *flirty*. Her lack of confidence had her standing on the dating sidelines when she was dying to be in the game. . . . She just didn't quite know how to play.

Halley glanced up and smiled when she spotted her brother entering the bar. "Your turn," she said, and nudged Jenna's leg under the table. "Get ready—Cole's coming our way."

Jenna gasped. "No! I need to freshen up. Halley, you stall him while I go to the ladies' room."

"We'll go with you," Cathy and Sallie offered, and then slid out of the booth.

"Hi, Cole," Halley said when he made it over to the table. Dressed casually in faded jeans and a green golf shirt, he drew attention without even trying.

He cocked a dark eyebrow. "What, did I scare your friends away?" He motioned for the waiter. "What are you guys drinking? I'll buy a round."

"Just light beers."

Cole nodded and placed the order. "Now tell me—where did your friends run off to?"

Halley grinned. "The ladies' room."

"Right, I forgot. Girls pee in groups." He paid the waiter who returned with the round, and tilted back his beer. "So, are you having fun?"

Halley nodded, but then leaned across the table and said quietly, "I need your help, and if you blow this, I'll kick your butt."

chapter three

Cole set his beer bottle down with a clunk. "Let me get this straight. You want me to ask Jenna to dance, and then kiss her, making sure your friends can see?"

"It's just a bachelorette game we're playing. To get a kiss from our fantasy man."

"I'm Jenna's fantasy?" He gave her a cocky grin and then took a long swallow of his beer.

"Don't you dare tell her I told you that! And Cole, I'm talking just one little bitty kiss. She's my friend and I don't want you to mess with her."

Cole's grin remained, setting her teeth on edge.

"I mean it. I'm only asking because I know she won't have the nerve to do this on her own. One dance, one kiss."

"You act like she's Little Red Riding Hood and I'm the big bad wolf."

"Well, that's a pretty good description. You could gobble her up."

"Wow, I think I like this. She *is* kinda cute."

"Cole . . ."

He put his palms up in surrender. "Okay. I'll be good and play your little bachelorette game. Hey, who is *your* fantasy?"

Halley felt a blush creep up her neck.

"Tell me or I won't kiss Jenna."

Halley gasped. "You don't play fair!"

He folded his arms across his chest and waited.

Halley saw her friends heading back from the ladies' room. "All right," she muttered quickly. "The black guy at the bar."

Frowning, Cole glanced in the direction of the bar. "Reese Taylor?"

"Y-yes." She was sure her face was flaming. "You know him?"

"Just casually. He's a hellava pitcher, but a hothead and a real ladies' man, Halley. I don't think you should mess with him."

Halley narrowed her eyes at Cole. "You don't think I can do it, do you?"

Cole shook his head. "I didn't mean that he wouldn't find you attractive. I just think he isn't your type."

Halley opened her mouth to argue, but her friends interrupted.

"Hello, ladies." He scooted over so they could sit down. "I bought you a round."

Jenna quickly slid into the booth next to Halley instead of by Cole. *Good Lord*, thought Halley, *the girl is already practically swooning. If Cole kisses her, she just might faint.* With that thought, she nudged him hard with her toe under the table. He looked at her and she tried to convey with her eyes that he *not* go through with their plan, but being a guy, he misinterpreted her cue.

After a little bit of small talk, Cole smoothly asked, "Jenna, I feel like dancing, and I seem to remember you're good at it. Care to join me?"

Her mouth dropped open and she blinked at him several times. "Ah, sure." She slid from the booth and followed him to the dance floor.

"Ohmygod!" Cathy squeaked, and angled her body toward the action.

Halley groaned. As if on cue, the band decided to play a sultry, slow song.

"She'll never kiss him," Sallie said, but kept her gaze on them, anyway.

Halley watched with her hands clasped under the table. The dance floor wasn't too crowded, so they had a clear view of Cole and Jenna swaying slowly to the love song. The top of Jenna's head just reached Cole's chin. She looked tiny and feminine in her yellow sundress, which brushed against her bare legs as they moved. His hands rested lightly on her waist, and Halley noted with relief that there were several inches between them.

But then Jenna glanced in their direction as if telling them to watch. Her hands rested on his shoulders, but she suddenly inched closer to Cole and wrapped her arms around his neck.

"Wow," Sallie said. "Our little Jenna might just surprise us."

A good dancer, Cole led her around the floor. With no space between them now, Cole moved one hand to her bare back. Jenna tilted her head up, almost brushing his lips.

"She's gonna do it," Sallie said, but the song ended. The couples started to walk off the floor. "Guess not . . . oh!"

They watched Cole as he thanked her for the dance and leaned down to give her what looked like a quick kiss, but Jenna pulled his head down and gave him a lingering lip-lock to remember.

Halley watched the look on Cole's face when Jenna smiled shyly up at him and put a hand coyly over her mouth . . . and it wasn't Jenna who looked ready to melt. Cole gazed down at her for a long moment, looking a little stunned, and Halley had to grin. Jenna leaned in close to his ear and told him something. A look of disappointment flickered across his handsome features, but he quickly recovered and followed Jenna back to the table.

Flushed, and looking a bit pleased with herself, Jenna sat down and gestured for Cole to join them.

"I won't crash your party, ladies," Cole said with a grin.

Halley noticed that his gaze lingered for a moment on Jenna as if he might say something to her, but then he gave them a wave and walked away.

"Wow, Jenna," said Sallie. "I'm impressed. Fifty percent off is yours, sister." She poured beer into her glass and then surveyed the crowded bar. "Now *I* need to find my muscle-bound hunk, and lay one on him."

"So, Jenna, did kissing my brother make your knees weak?"

"Like Jell-O," she said with a long sigh. "You know, sometimes you wait all your life for something, and when it happens, you're disappointed, ya know? Well, I wasn't disappointed." She shrugged. "I know nothing will come of it. I'm hardly in Cole's league, but oh, boy, being in his arms was heaven."

Halley knew her brother well enough to know he was affected by the kiss as much as Jenna, but she wasn't about to tell her friend that. Cole was a player, and she didn't want to see Jenna hurt by her womanizing brother.

"Hey, Cathy," Jenna said with a giggle, and pointed. "I see a butt I want you to pinch."

"That guy's old enough to be my father," Cathy protested.

Jenna shrugged. "Go do it, girlfriend."

"I'm going trolling for my hunk," Sallie announced as she slid from the bench seat. "If I'm not back in fifteen minutes, do *not* come looking for me."

Halley had to smile as she watched Sallie work the room. She chatted with Jenna about the wedding while Cathy zeroed in on her butt-pinching victim.

"Well," Jenna said after finishing her beer, "I need to use the bathroom."

"I'll go with you." Halley had just spotted Reese Taylor at the bar again. She wanted to freshen up before making her own move. The competitive edge in her nature wouldn't let her friends meet the crazy challenges without taking one of her own.

chapter four

Reese leaned against the bar and took a swallow of cold beer as he gazed up at the television suspended from the wall. ESPN rolled the major-league baseball scores across the bottom of the screen while showing highlights of the games.

With a grimace, he absently rolled his shoulder, trying to ease the dull throb in his left arm, a result of overpitching the night before. He had argued when Chase Mitchell wanted to pull him, and Chase had reluctantly left him in to finish the game. Pitching complete games would get him to the majors, but he had worked his arm too hard in the effort to get another win under his belt.

Reese pulled his gaze from the television and ordered another beer, thinking he would have one more before heading home. Pain shot through his arm when someone bumped him hard. "Damn," he said through gritted teeth, and turned around with a glare.

"Oh, I'm sorry. I—I was bumped from behind."

"No problem." His glare softened when he found himself lost in the depths of the prettiest pair of blue eyes he had ever seen. She was attractive in a girl-next-door kind of way that wasn't the bitchy love-'em-and-leave-'em high-maintenance women he usually went after.

Dark, fringy hair framed a sweet face that was more cute than beautiful . . . except for her mouth. *Damn.* She had a full, pouty mouth that begged to be kissed. And she was tall, just a few inches shorter than his own six feet two. Reese suddenly imagined those long legs wrapped around him . . . and then gave himself a mental shake. Her sweet face, trembling smile, screamed small-town innocence, so he turned his attention away from her.

"Oh!" She bumped into him again.

Hearing some shouts, Reese turned and caught her against him when he realized a fight had broken out directly behind them. Bouncers pounced and attempted to break up the fight. When a flying fist came dangerously close, Reese wrapped his arms around her, shielding her with his body. He felt her tense at the sound of flesh connecting with flesh.

"It's okay," he assured her with his mouth close to her ear. "The bouncers are dragging them out of here."

A few minutes later, the commotion died down, and he released his hold on her but remained close. "Are you okay?"

She nodded, but looked shaken.

"Let me buy you a drink."

She swallowed, and managed a small smile. "Sure, a light beer, please."

He motioned to the bartender and then handed her the cold bottle. Their fingers merely brushed, but he felt a slow burn of sexual heat that went straight to his groin.

"Thanks." She tipped the bottle up and took a sip.

She seemed nervous and he wondered if it was because he was black. His mother was a beautiful blonde and his father a black man, making it hard for him to decide exactly *what* he was. His parents shared a love that most people only dreamed about, and ignored the lingering prejudice and disapproval of those with narrow minds . . . but Reese wasn't so forgiving. Racial slurs had gotten him into many fights over the years, and he carried a chip on his shoulder that he just could not shake.

"Are you here with someone?" Reese asked, not wanting to get into a fight of his own. Chase Mitchell, the team manager, would have a fit.

"Just some girlfriends." She grinned. "A bachelorette party, but I think I'm ready to call it a night."

"Oh, by the way, I'm Reese Taylor."

"Halley Forrester."

"Related to Cole?"

"My brother. I guess you know him for the promo work his agency does for the Flyers."

Reese nodded. "You like baseball?"

She nodded and gave him a grin that showed a cute dimple in her cheek. "I'm a sports *nut*. I teach phys ed over at Sander's High. I've been to a few Flyers games with Erin Manning, the school principal."

"Ah, married to Michael Manning. That man had a curveball to die for."

"I'd love to see you pitch."

"I'll get you tickets whenever you want them." He could have bit his tongue. She was so sweet, so *not* his type. He should just shut his mouth and run in the other direction. She was just too nice to get involved with a badass like him.

"Halley?" A dark-haired bombshell approached them. "We've decided to let Cathy and Rob have the limo for the rest of the night. He called her on her cell, and we thought it would be fun for the bride-groom-to-be. Cole offered to drive us home."

"Are you leaving soon?" Halley asked.

"Not for a while."

"I can give you a ride home, Halley," Reese offered, and could have kicked his own ass for the eagerness in his voice.

"Oh, Sallie, I'm sorry—this is Reese Taylor."

"Nice to meet you," Sallie said, and shook his hand.

Halley looked up at him and he half hoped she would refuse. "I live over in the Ridgeview apartment complex. Is that out of your way?"

"Not at all." It was the opposite direction.

"Well, okay, then, if you're sure."

He was sure he would kiss that pouty mouth before the night was over. "Yeah, no problem."

She smiled. "Just let me say good night to my friends."

Reese nodded and followed her over to a booth across the room. As she said good-bye to her friends, he felt an undercurrent of something going on, but decided it was just a chick thing.

He led her across the parking lot to his SUV and opened the door for her. As she climbed in, he caught a glimpse of long, tan legs as she tugged at her white skirt.

During the short ride across town, he tried to decide whether to press for an invitation up to her place. It had been a long time since he had felt this strong of an attraction to a woman. She was the type of girl he could hurt, yet his intense desire needed some relief.

"I'm in Building 302, over there," she said, pointing when they pulled into the complex.

"Gotcha." Reese pulled into a parking space and was surprised to find that his heart was thudding. "Does your place overlook the Ohio River?" he asked in an effort to make small talk. Reese *never* made small talk. He liked to get to the point.

"Yes," she replied with a smile in his direction. "I pay two hundred dollars extra that I can't afford for the view, but I tell myself it's worth eating chicken noodle soup on a regular basis."

Reese killed the engine, wanting to prolong his time with her a few minutes longer, but had decided not to pursue an invitation. Once he stepped into her place, he would be all over her in nothing flat. And although he sensed she was the "good girl," hometown type, he knew he could get her into bed.

He always could. The combined genes of his parents, his father being a powerful athlete and his mother a beautiful woman, had rolled him into a package that few women could resist . . . but that was as deep as it went. He was good enough for a thorough fuck, but it seemed that black women didn't find him black enough, and white women didn't find him white enough.

While he was never hurting for a woman to share his bed, he often wondered if he would ever find a woman to share his life.

"Would you like to come up for a nightcap?"

"Sure." The word tumbled out of his mouth, answering the call of his dick, when his brain knew full well it was a big mistake.

chapter five

Halley fumbled with the keys to her door, dropped them once, and finally managed to insert one from the jangling mess into the lock. Butterflies in the stomach, weak knees, being tongue-tied, were mild sensations compared with the confusion in her befuddled brain.

So *this* was what it felt like to be captivated by a guy.

She flicked on the light when they entered a short hallway flanked by a half bath on one side and a closet on the other. She could feel his presence right behind her, smell his spicy cologne.

"Make yourself at home," she offered with a wave of her hand toward the small living room. Flicking on another light, she entered the galley-style kitchen, separated from the rest of the room by a small breakfast bar. "What can I get for you? Beer, soft drink, or bottled water?" She felt nervous as she smiled at him . . . *excited* . . . and incredibly turned on.

"Water is fine." He walked over to the sliding glass door that opened to a small patio. "It's too dark to see, but I'm guessing this overlooks the river?"

Halley nodded. "Yes," she replied as she crossed the room and then handed him the cold bottle. "I've always been drawn to the water. Oceans, lakes, rivers . . . even the rain."

He unscrewed the cap and took a long drink. Halley watched his Adam's apple move and let her gaze follow the long column of his throat to where his shirt showed a small vee of dark skin. He was quite simply . . . gorgeous. With skin the color of her morning coffee, deep-set brown eyes, and beautiful bone structure, he was enough to make her drift toward him in silent invitation.

Her unopened water bottle slipped from her fingers and landed on the carpet with a muted thump. With his gaze never leaving her face, he set his own bottle down and wrapped his hands around her waist, pulling her against the hard length of his body.

Tipping his head forward, he leaned in and kissed her. His lips were firm but soft, and his mouth was wet from his drink of water. Halley sank into the kiss, welcoming the thrust of his tongue. Her arms reached up and encircled his neck, and she loved the feel of her breasts crushed against his chest. The steely hardness of his erection made her moan into his mouth. Needing to feel his bare skin, she slid her hands from his neck, down his back, and tugged at his shirt until she had it untucked. She moved her hands underneath the soft cotton, feeling the smooth heat of his skin, the ripple of muscle.

Finally breaking the kiss, he murmured into her ear, "Do you want me to take it off?"

"What?" Dazed, her legs felt like Jell-O.

With a low chuckle, he led her over to the couch and pulled her down with him. "My shirt. I'll take it off for you."

The thought of his naked chest beneath her hands, her mouth, had her shaking. This whole thing felt surreal. "Take it off." She couldn't be doing this . . . and yet she was.

She watched him pull the shirt over his head and toss it to the floor in one fluid motion. Light filtered in from the kitchen, casting a warm glow over his bare torso. He leaned back against the plump blue pillows and let her look her fill. Lean and muscled, he had defined pecs and washboard abs.

"You can touch," he offered, and grabbed her hand, placing it against his chest.

With a quick intake of breath, Halley leaned forward, bracing herself against the couch with one hand while her other hand trailed over his chest. Lightly, she let her fingertips graze his warm flesh. The rippled ridges of his stomach quivered while she explored. When her fingers reached the top of his pants, she looked up and met the heat of his gaze.

"Reese, what's happening here?"

"I think you know."

"I—" She swallowed. He was giving her a choice. Her heart thudded. Things like this just didn't happen to her.

"I should go." He smiled softly at her and tucked a strand of her hair behind her ear.

Halley's eyes fluttered shut at his unexpected, tender gesture. Reese Taylor, she knew, was labeled a hothead. Cole had just warned her that he was a player, certainly *not* her type, and she should send him on his way . . .

But then she felt the warm softness of his lips against her own. Unable to resist, she opened her mouth for him, giving, and then taking. With a sigh of surrender, she melted against him.

In one easy move, he lifted her onto his lap, cradling her head with one hand while kissing her senseless. His other hand skimmed up her leg, underneath her skirt, stopping just short of where she burned for his touch. She squirmed, and his hand inched up her thigh until his fingertips touched the edge of her panties. With a groan, his mouth left her lips and began a hot trail of kisses down her neck. Halley angled her head, giving him access to her neck and the swell of her breasts above her scoop neck T-shirt.

She gasped when his mouth found her nipple. Through the cotton of her shirt and the silk of her bra, his teeth tugged, sending a sharp sizzle of heat that had her arching her back, filling his mouth with her softness. "Reese!" His name sounded like a ragged plea . . . and it was.

chapter six

If there were two things in life Reese knew well, they were how to pitch a baseball and how to pleasure a woman. At one point he realized there were some similarities: knowing when to go hard and fast, and when to go slow, when to bear down, and when to pull back. Rhythm, instinct, and knowing who you were up against all played into the game . . . and for Reese, women, like baseball, were nothing more than a game to be played and enjoyed.

Reese eased his fingertip just underneath the elastic of her panties, and she shivered. He wanted to slip his finger inside her and make her come.

But he didn't.

"I should go," he told her again.

She looked up at him, her blue eyes dark with need. "I don't want you to leave." She placed her palm lightly against his chest and then softly pleaded, "Don't go, Reese."

He looked at her through half-lidded eyes, taking in her sweet trembling smile, mouth swollen from his kisses, and felt something stir inside him. He had a small-town schoolteacher in his arms. She radiated a sexy sweetness that was so natural, so unpretentious.

She was *nothing* like any woman he had ever had, and *everything* he truly wanted. They had met by chance, and a voice inside his head told him to go for it. This could mean something.

"Stay," she repeated.

When Reese would have refused, she reached up and cupped his cheek in her hand and *he was lost.* "Halley—" he began, but she put a silencing finger to his lips.

"I know what you're thinking, and you're right. This isn't something that I do."

Reese gently put his hand around her wrist, kissed her finger, and reluctantly said, "And that's why I'm not going to let you do it."

She angled her head, causing strands of dark hair to tickle across his chest. "You don't want to . . . to . . ." She blushed and averted her gaze.

Reese tilted her chin up with the tip of his finger. "Make love to you?"

She nodded, catching her full bottom lip between her teeth.

"Baby, I want you more than a strikeout with the bases loaded, but you're too much of a sweetheart for a badass like me. And I know you've been partying with those girlfriends of yours." He sighed. "I'd hate to see regret in those beautiful blue eyes of yours, so I'm going to leave."

"You are a gentleman, Reese Taylor." She gave him a trembling smile that turned him inside out.

"Come here," he said gruffly, and leaning back against the cushions, he pulled her up against his chest. "Kiss me one last time before I go."

"Okay," she said softly. Wrapping her arms around his neck, she lowered her head, but when her mouth met his, he knew that asking for the kiss had been a mistake. Sweet, unpracticed, almost tentative, her mouth moved against his lips softly . . . and set him on fire. He was no stranger to desire, but this . . . *this* was a sweet longing, a deep pull that had him wrapping his arms around her, holding her close, and kissing her back like there was no tomorrow.

With a little hitching moan that came from the back of her throat, she moved against him, just a slight rock with her hips against his hard cock, and he thought he was going to come in his boxers like a teenager. He pulled his mouth from hers and inhaled a shaky breath that filled his head with her scent.

"God, Halley."

"Reese, I'm sorry. You're trying to be a gentleman and I'm throwing myself at you." She splayed her hands on his chest and closed her eyes as if in shame. "I can't believe I'm acting this way."

"Hey, look at me."

She opened her eyes.

"I asked for the kiss, remember?" He tucked a wayward strand of dark, silky hair behind her ear and smiled when she nodded. "And just for the record, I'm no gentleman, Halley. That's why I'm leaving before—"

She reached up and put her finger to his lips. "I would *not* regret making love to you, but we should take things a little slower. Come over tomorrow after your game and I'll cook dinner for you."

Reese hesitated.

Halley put her hand to her mouth and pushed away from him. "Oh, you don't want to see me again." She rolled her eyes while shaking her head. "You offer me a simple ride home, and I make embarrassing assumptions."

"The Flyers are off tomorrow," he said with a slow smile. "I'll bring the wine." God, as soon as he accepted, he wanted to back out. He was all wrong for her, but her face lit up with such a bright smile that he couldn't back out.

"Bring a bottle of Chianti. I'll do Italian if that's okay with you."

"Pasta is great since I pitch on Monday. I always do pasta before a game."

"Perfect." She reached down, picked up his discarded shirt, and handed it to him with a shy smile.

Reese tugged it over his head and shoved his arms through the sleeves. He could feel her eyes upon him and found himself inordinately pleased that she admired his body. Although he was used to female admiration, took it for granted really, her gaze turned him on . . . made him want to flex his muscles like a caveman.

God help her if they made love. He would be insatiable.

She led him to the door, but he was reluctant to leave. Suddenly, tomorrow night seemed too long of a wait to see her again. Pausing, he searched his brain for the small talk that he was so bad at. "I'll bring dessert," he blurted out, but she grinned, putting him at ease.

"Something sinfully chocolate, please."

He wanted to give her a sexy, cocky comeback, but the thought of rich, dark chocolate melting in her mouth made him lose his train of thought. So instead, he leaned over and kissed her. A naughty thought popped into his sex-befuddled brain and to his horror, he said it out loud. "Mmmm, I could always just put whipped cream on you."

She looked at him for a long moment. Reese wanted to put the heel of his hand to his head and apologize for the crass remark. Geez, he usually was a bit smoother than *that*. He felt like a real cheese ball and wanted the floor to swallow him up.

And then she giggled.

A blush crept from Reese's neck to his face and he hoped his dark skin hid his embarrassment. She giggled harder . . . not one of those irritating giggles, but a sexy low in the throat rumble that was infectious. He joined her laughter and soon had to lean back against the wall while holding his sides.

"God," he finally managed. "I'm such a dork."

Her eyebrows shot up. "What? You've got to be kidding." She angled her head and gave him a smile that had him imagining the whipped-cream scenario all over again. "I think you are adorable."

Reese had been called many things in his twenty-five years on earth, but had never been called adorable. It just didn't fit. His mother—God love her for putting up with him—had probably never even called him adorable. He *knew* his father hadn't. He had been hell on wheels as a toddler, and never looked back. He had perfected the snarl, the lethal glare, that made ballplayers cringe, step out of the batter's box, and spit nervously in the dirt.

"You gotta be kidding."

chapter seven

"I'm serious. You *are* adorable, but it'll be our little secret." When he snorted, Halley wanted to tell him that she could see right through his bad-boy act. She knew the drill. Her brother, Cole, was the same way. Bad to the bone on the outside, but he would give you the shirt off of his back. . . . Sheesh . . . that thought conjured up the recent sight of Reese shirtless, and she suddenly felt the need to fan her face.

"Ahh, Halley, when you look at me like that, it sure makes it hard to leave."

Then don't, was on the tip of her tongue, but the sensible schoolteacher in her won out. Sleeping with a stranger wasn't her style, even though he didn't feel like a stranger to her. Everything about him felt right, but she needed to slow things down. "I'll see you around seven tomorrow?"

He nodded, and for a heart-pounding moment, she

thought he was going to kiss her again, but instead he turned toward the door. She let him out, shut the door with a soft click. With a little moan she leaned against the cool wood, and slid on shaky legs to the floor. With her head in her hands she thought wildly that she had almost slept with him! And while she wasn't a virgin, she had never, ever gotten caught up in the moment like that . . . but then again, no man had ever made her feel that way . . . like she was melting.

For a few moments, she simply sat there and relived the feel of his mouth, his hands, the deep timbre of his voice. The masculine spice of his cologne hung faintly in the air and she breathed deeply, savoring the scent. Tomorrow couldn't come soon enough.

The next morning, Halley woke up with the birds singing outside her open bedroom window. Shivering in the early-morning chill, she snuggled under the covers and decided to sleep for a while longer, an indulgence she allowed herself during the weeks of summer when school was out.

And then she remembered. Reese Taylor was coming to dinner. She had so much to do in so little time. Throwing back the covers, she hurried to the bathroom, her bare feet slapping against the hardwood floor. Mentally, she ticked off all the things she needed to do before seven o'clock: shop for her dinner, prepare her homemade marinara sauce, clean her apartment . . . and oh, God, what was she going to wear?

Halley opened her closet door and rummaged around for a few minutes and found nothing . . . *nothing!* Everything was too schoolteacherish. Too outdated. She wanted something flirty, sexy. Okay, she'd add shopping for a kick-ass outfit to her list.

After a quick shower, she grabbed a breakfast bar and headed out the door with a list clutched in her hand. Halley was a firm believer in lists. Be prepared, be on time, and everything will go smoothly. Halley liked things orderly. Chaos made her crazy. Perhaps that was why she felt so nervous about this dinner with Reese, she thought as she pulled her blue sedan into a vacant spot at the mall. Her invitation to him had been totally unexpected.

She grinned and pushed the lock button. *Unexpected.* Maybe that was part of the allure. For a moment, she angled her head at her sensible car; glanced down at her sensible sneakers, conservative khakis, and sweater set; and decided it was time for a change.

Sexy Reese Taylor had unleashed her sensuality, made her want to throw caution to the wind and live a little. Shoving the door to the mall open, she lifted her chin a notch. "Look out," she said softly when she really wanted to shout to the world, "Halley Forrester, small-town schoolteacher, is about to let her hair down." That thought put a spring in her step and a saucy smile on her face. She had a credit card that she paid off every month . . . and she suddenly felt like doing some serious damage.

Halley boldly walked into an expensive little boutique that she usually avoided and was immediately approached by a chic salesclerk.

"May I help you?" she asked with a bright smile.

Halley returned the smile. "I'm looking for something . . . ah . . . feminine, a little flirty."

"You mean sexy?"

A little heat crept into Halley's cheeks. "Yes."

"Hmmm." She tapped her finger against her cheek. "I'm guessing you are about a size eight?"

Halley nodded.

"Follow me."

Fifteen minutes later, Halley was in a large dressing room with about a dozen outfits, mostly strappy little dresses. *When* was the last time she had worn a dress? She rarely wore them, even as a child. Being raised by her brother and father, she was always a tomboy, never feeling comfortable in frills. What she had learned about her period, makeup, and boys had come from her friends, one of the reasons she valued them so much. Her father never even gave her the standard sex talk. The only advice she had gotten was just before her junior prom, when Cole had pulled her aside and said, "If he tries to get in your pants, kick him in the balls."

After slipping the first dress on, she stepped back and gazed at her reflection in the mirror. "Oh, my," she breathed. Made of cream-colored silk, the simple halter design bared her shoulders, and flared just above the knee. When she turned, the skirt twirled slightly, and then caressed her legs. A dress made to dance in . . . not that she was much of a dancer.

Halley imagined herself dancing cheek to cheek with Reese, and a thought hit her. Tonight, she would ask him to Cathy's wedding. Forcing herself not to look at the price tag, she carefully removed the dress and hung it on a hook. After the first dress, however, she struck out. She tossed one after the other to the side. Too clingy, too tight, too big, too small, wrong color, too *ugly*! Ugh, made her butt look huge, her boobs too small. She was hanging them all back up when there was a light tap on the door.

"Yes?" Still in her underwear, Halley opened the door and peeked around it.

The perky salesclerk handed her a dress. "I found this on the sale rack. With your dark hair, I thought this color would look awesome on you. And it is *definitely* sexy."

"Thank you," Halley accepted.

"Let me see it after you try it on."

Halley stepped into the little dress and zipped it up at the side. A simple strapless sheath, it hit a few inches above the knee. Made of rayon, the material felt cool and silky, clinging slightly to her curves. The salesclerk was right. . . . The lavender shade was perfect for her coloring, showing off her early summer tan.

"May I see?"

Halley opened the door. Catching her bottom lip with her teeth, she looked at her expectantly. "What do you think?"

"Your boyfriend is going to love it. You look hot. That dress is *you*."

"Is it too dressy for dinner at my house?"

"Oh, no. You can dress it up with pearls or wear it to a picnic. It's perfect."

"You think?"

"Turn around."

Halley turned while looking at the clerk over her shoulder.

"Ah, just make sure you wear a thong. The rayon

clings a bit to your bum. You don't want panty lines. Wear a strapless push-up bra and your boyfriend will have trouble swallowing his food."

Halley's eyes widened. "I . . . ah, don't have one of those things."

"Things?"

"Thongs."

"Sugar, I can hook you up."

Fifteen minutes later, Halley left the shop with the two dresses, three thongs, and a bra that made her boobs look plump and inviting. The question remained: Would she have the nerve to wear them?

The rest of the morning was spent shopping for dinner ingredients. After arriving back at her apartment, she made her sauce and then cleaned while the aroma of garlic and basil made her mouth water. By late afternoon, she had everything ready . . . the salad tossed, the lasagna put together, and the table set. With a contented sigh, she looked around for any imperfection.

The apartment complex was rather old, but Halley liked the charm of the hardwood floors, the dated cabinets and light fixtures. Her furniture was an eclectic mixture of antique and garage sale treasures that Sallie called "country chic." Halley knew only that she liked dark, polished wood, overstuffed chairs, rich jewel tones.

Everything done, she decided to take a long soak in the bathtub. Her heart skipped a beat when she thought of Reese arriving. She couldn't remember when she had anticipated an evening more.

chapter
eight

Reese put the heel of his hand to his head and closed his eyes. "What in the hell was I thinking? She's a small-town schoolteacher with innocent eyes and a body made for sin." He stood in his kitchen with a towel wrapped around his waist, still damp from a shower. He glanced down at the tent in the towel and moaned. God, just thinking about her made him hard.

She wouldn't be casual sex; he just knew it. She was already under his skin . . . his *black* skin. How would the small-town folks take to one of their own dating a black ballplayer with a bad reputation? Rubbing his hand over his damp, close-cropped hair, he marveled for the millionth time how his mother and father never let prejudice bother them. They ignored the stares, the whispers, that they still got even in this day and age.

Reese yanked the door to his refrigerator open and

snagged a beer. With a quick twist, he opened the bottle and took a long swig. Hell, he thought, maybe she would be relieved if he canceled. After all, she had been drinking last night. Maybe this morning she had regrets about inviting him over.

He looked her number up in the phone book, picked up the phone, and then with a curse slammed it back on the cradle. Closing his eyes, he took a deep breath. He wanted to see her again. He drained the beer, tossed the empty bottle in the trash, and then headed to his bedroom to get dressed.

He chose a light blue oxford shirt, soft gray dress slacks and loafers . . . understated, not I-want-to-get-laid clothes. Even though he wanted to get laid. Bad. But he wouldn't. He would have dinner with her, but end it tonight. He was in this town to make it to the major leagues. Damn it, he needed to focus, not get tangled up with a woman.

And then he remembered how it felt to have her in his arms, the sweet taste of her mouth, and the tickle of her silky hair against his bare skin. *Damn.* That was it. He stalked across the room, picked up the phone, and dialed her number.

"Hello."

Reese hesitated. The sound of her soft, sultry voice made him pause.

"Hello?" she repeated.

Ah . . . fuck it. "Halley? It's Reese."

"Oh, hi!"

He winced and gripped the phone tighter. "I can't make it tonight."

"Oh . . ." Her voice dropped an octave. She waited

for an explanation, but he hadn't thought that far ahead.

"Sorry," he said lamely.

Silence.

"Well, I'll—"

"Don't say you'll call me. It's . . . it's okay." *Click.*

"Fuck, fuck, *fuck.*" He thought about calling her back with some sort of lie, but couldn't bring himself to hear the waver in her voice. *It's better this way,* he thought. *Let her know she's lucky not to get involved with an asshole like me.* He chuckled darkly. "Babe, you're better off."

Halley blinked at the phone as if it were something evil. "I will not cry." But then she looked across the room at the tapered candles, the fresh spring bouquet, the pretty table setting, and her mouth trembled. She snagged a wine goblet and then on wooden legs went into the kitchen and uncorked a bottle of Chianti. Pouring herself a generous portion, she took a sip of wine that mixed with hot tears, clogging her throat.

With a sniff and a determined lift of her chin, she took her wine and headed to the sliding glass doors that led to the back patio. She sat down in a canvas chair and looked out on the river view. A cool summer breeze caressed her bare shoulders and ruffled her hair that had taken her thirty minutes to tame into a French twist. She shivered but remained there for a while, watching the sunset and nursing her wine.

When her stomach rumbled in protest, she headed back inside, deciding that her dinner shouldn't be wasted. But when she opened the oven door and saw the bubbling lasagna, she knew she couldn't stomach it. With a sigh, she turned the oven off, picked up a crusty roll, and nibbled at it without enthusiasm. "Men," she grumbled.

The more she thought about being stood up, the angrier she got. When the doorbell chimed, she stomped across the room on high heels that pinched her toes but looked sexy. She hoped her brother or father, the paperboy . . . *someone* sporting a penis was on the other side of the door so she could tell him just how much men sucked.

She swung open the door, prepared to vent, but it was eighty-year-old Mr. Parker from three doors down. Yes, she supposed he had a wrinkled old penis, but such a kind smile that she couldn't bear to be bitchy to him.

His shaggy gray eyebrows rose. "My, my, Miss Halley. Don't you look pretty?"

Halley looked down at her pushed-up breasts and felt heat creep up her neck. As soon as Mr. Parker left, she was going to change into her sweatpants. Forever.

"Can I get something for you, Mr. Parker?"

He frowned, still blinking at her breasts, and then snapped his fingers. "An egg. The missus is making brownies, and we need an egg."

"I'll get an egg for you," Halley offered, and winced when he followed her into her apartment.

He looked over at the elegantly set table and gave a low whistle. "Ahh, hot date, Miss Halley?"

She ground her teeth together. "Here's your egg, Mr. Parker." She was coming dangerously close to venting her opinion of the male population, so she quickly shooed him out the door.

A moment later, she was heading to her bedroom to change into sweats when the doorbell chimed again. If it was Mr. Parker, she was going to crack an egg on his bald head. She marched back over to the door, managing to painfully turn an ankle in the damned high heels. "Owww!" She reached for the door handle with one hand while bending over to remove the shoe with her other.

"Halley?"

The sound of Reese's deep voice had her quickly looking up with her finger hooked in the strap of her shoe. She promptly lost her balance, landing with a thud on her butt, causing her artfully arranged hair to come loose and cascade to her shoulders. Talk about adding insult to injury . . .

"Are you okay?"

Halley looked up with a glare. He filled the doorway, looking down at her with a frown, so she did what any pissed woman would do. She threw her shoe at him. Of course being a baseball player, he caught it before it could do any physical damage, like knock him out. "Go away," she said childishly, and was dangerously close to tears.

"Let me help you up," he offered, reaching his hand toward her.

Halley slapped his hand away and ungracefully got up. She put unbalanced weight on her twisted ankle. With a cry of pain, she fell forward.

"Whoa." Reese caught her around the waist.

She pushed at his chest. "Let me go."

"You're hurt."

"I'm fine."

"The hell you are." He scooped her up into his arms and nudged the door shut with his elbow.

"Put me down!" She struggled, but his muscled arms held her firmly. With a sigh, she gave up and asked him, "Why are you here?"

"I couldn't stay away."

"Oh." Her anger evaporated like a drop of summer rain on a hot sidewalk. Her arms were linked around his neck, and his face was mere inches from hers. She looked into his deep brown eyes and was lost. He thought he was such a badass, but all she could see was vulnerability. She released one hand from around his neck and rubbed her palm over the dark stubble of his cheek. Then, with her fingertip, she traced the fullness of his bottom lip.

She felt the muscles tighten in his biceps, and his eyelids fluttered shut. "Halley, don't—"

She smothered his protest by covering his mouth with hers. He groaned and tried to pull back, but she held his cheeks with her hands. Still, he resisted, so she nibbled softly on his bottom lip, and then traced the tip of her tongue over his mouth, urging, seeking, until he gave in and opened for her.

Shyly, she slid her tongue into his mouth. He was

heat, strength, power. Her heart pounded, and she deepened the kiss, loving the feel of him, the taste of him. She could have kissed him forever, but she felt his arms tremble and reluctantly pulled her mouth from his.

"I'm too heavy."

"No way."

"But you're trembling."

He leaned his forehead against hers. "That's not the reason." He sighed and then chuckled weakly. "Let me see that ankle of yours." He carried her over to the sofa and gently put her down. Kneeling down next to the cushions, he examined her foot.

"It's not too bad. I just turned it slightly."

Reese removed the other sandal and let the strappy thing dangle from his finger. He shook his head. "These things are dangerous."

"I wore them for you."

"Halley—"

"And the dress. I *never* wear dresses. I'm not much of a girlie girl."

With raised eyebrows he looked down at her breasts spilling over the top of the dress. Her mouth was moist and shiny from kissing him, and her dark hair tumbled around her shoulders with a just-laid look. "I've never seen a sexier woman in my life."

She blushed, reminding him of her sweetness. She had an innocent quality about her, but he somehow knew she'd be wild in bed. He'd make her wild. Reese took a deep, shaky breath. But that wasn't why he came to her. He just couldn't stand the thought that he'd hurt her by standing her up. He'd meant only to apologize and then leave.

"Don't you even think about leaving."

Reese was floored that she could read him so well. "Halley, there are issues—"

She reached up and put a finger to his lips. "I know what you're thinking and it doesn't matter."

Reese knew better, but let it go for now. "Let me serve dinner. You stay off of that foot." He put a pillow under her calf and headed for the kitchen.

"The salad is in the fridge," she called from the living room.

"Gotcha."

"And the lasagna's warming in the oven."

He topped off her wineglass and brought it to her. "I've got it under control. Let me wait on you."

She took a sip of wine and eyed him over the rim of her goblet. "So, I get to order you around?"

He grinned. "Yeah."

"Okay, kiss me."

His grin faded. "Halley . . ."

"One little kiss."

He removed her glass from her hand and took a sip. Then kneeling down, he leaned over, meaning to give her a brief kiss, but the second his mouth touched hers he had to have more. Her hand reached up to touch his cheek and something inside him softened.

This was a woman he could fall deeply in love with.

"Let's eat dinner," he said gruffly. He was confused. This wasn't going the way he had planned . . . but maybe deep down he had known he would stay.

He carried her over to the table and helped her into a chair. After he sat down across from her, he leaned down and lifted her ankle onto his lap. "You should keep it elevated to keep the swelling down."

She nodded and they began eating. They talked about sports and he was impressed with her knowledge.

"Don't look so surprised," she said with a grin. "I am a phys ed teacher, Reese. Plus, I grew up with an older brother and no mother. I had to learn sports." She shrugged. "I was never a Barbie doll kinda girl."

He sensed a bit of sadness and said, "You're my kinda girl."

Her blue eyes widened and Reese could have kicked himself. He was saying all the right things . . . and shouldn't.

"How about you? Do you have any siblings?"

Reese grinned. "I was hell on wheels. After me, I guess my mom and dad decided that one was enough." *My mother would like you,* he thought, but refrained from saying it.

"I bet they're proud of you."

"They are," he admitted, and took a sip of wine. "My mother always believed in me, but my dad didn't think I had the discipline to make it to the majors. I was always screwing off." Reese shrugged. "He still might be right. I can be a real head case."

"Why is that?" She angled her head at him and waited.

Reese toyed with the stem of his glass while trying to decide whether to give her a standard flippant comeback or to tell her the truth. The honest interest in her blue eyes had him sipping his wine instead of answering. She was pulling him in with her sweetness, her caring. She was everything he wanted . . . needed.

And should stay away from.

He decided to tell her the truth. Honesty would surely scare her the hell away . . . and that's what he wanted to do before things got way too complicated.

chapter
nine

Halley watched his long fingers play with the stem of the glass and waited. Emotion that he was trying hard to hide suddenly surfaced. She held her breath.

"Halley, you don't want to get tangled up with me."

She let out a shaky breath. That wasn't what she expected him to say. "I want to get tangled up with you in more ways than one."

His eyes widened at her unexpected candor and she saw a ghost of a smile. "You surprise me. You seem so shy and then . . ."

"Reese, I'm tougher than you think. I know what you're thinking. If we were in a restaurant right now, we'd be getting a few looks. I know that. I don't care."

He shook his head. "Easier said—"

"Reese—"

"No, listen. I'm the product of a mixed marriage, Halley. My dad is a successful lawyer. I grew up in an upper-class neighborhood with a bunch of rich, white kids."

"And you didn't fit in?"

He shrugged. "Yes, the weird thing is that I pretty much did. I grew up sheltered with liberal rich people in California. The race thing really didn't matter. It wasn't until college that I got hit in the face with the race thing. I wasn't white enough for white women or black enough for black women. I didn't fit in with the black baseball players, who mostly grew up under different circumstances. I was . . . lost. I got angry, confused. My parents never let that shit get to them, but I'm not so levelheaded." He shook his head. "You don't need this bullshit in your life. Go find some hometown boy."

Halley jammed her thumb in the direction of the door. "Then go."

"What?"

"You heard me. If that's what you think of me, then go." Angry, Halley pushed back from the table and tugged her foot from his lap. She stood up and hobbled toward the kitchen.

Reese caught up to her in two long strides. "This isn't about you. You're too sweet for someone screwed up like me."

Halley whirled around to face him, ignoring the pain in her ankle. "Then go," she repeated, but landed off-balance against him. He stabilized her by grabbing her upper arms. She was angry . . . but saddened because she knew he had a point. Tongues in the small town would wag; her father's eyebrows would rise.

But mostly she was disappointed with him for not

wanting to take the chance that they could make it work. Because she felt in her heart that it would be worth it.

He would be worth it.

And God, the man needed her. She could feel it in his gaze, his touch. "Go, Reese. I'll find a hometown boy and you go find a bimbo. No risk, no loss."

Still grasping her arms, he let his thumbs rub back and forth on her skin, causing a hot shiver of desire to shoot through her body.

Halley looked up and their eyes met, and held for a long moment. A muscle jumped in his jaw and then Halley did something she didn't think she had the nerve to do . . . but God, she had to. . . .

With her heart pumping, she reached up with trembling fingers and unzipped the side of her dress. The lavender material slid from her body and pooled onto the white tile floor. She took a step back, never letting her gaze stray from his.

"God, Halley," Reese breathed. He had been with beautiful women, but there was something almost painfully exquisite about her that took his breath away. Slender, she had a delicate look, but also the honed body of an athlete. The black lacy strapless bra pushed up her breasts like an offering to him, just barely covering her nipples, which strained against the material. He knew he could span her waist with his hands . . . and then, God, she was wearing a barely-there black thong. A little patch of silk coyly hiding where he suddenly needed to touch.

He reached out with his hand and ran one fingertip

over the silk. She was hot . . . damp. She gasped when he eased the fingertip underneath the edge of the thong, nearly grazing her soft mound.

"You want to do this, Halley?" His voice was a husky rasp, full of need.

"More than you can imagine."

With a growl, he picked her up. "Where's your bedroom?"

She pointed. "To the left." She buried her face in his neck, kissing, nibbling, and then began unbuttoning his shirt.

Reese found her bedroom, laid her gently on the double bed and then flicked on a small lamp on a nightstand. "You're beautiful."

She blushed.

"I want to see all of you."

"Okay." She nodded, and then reached up to unsnap her bra. Her breasts, small but perfection, tumbled out. Leaning over, he took one nipple into his mouth, laved it, and then suckled until she was arching up off of the bed. His hand found her thong. He cupped her there, finding the silk drenched.

Moving his mouth lower, he placed a trail of kisses over her quivering hot black silk, and then moved his tongue over the material.

She gasped, grabbed his head. "No . . . God, Reese, I'm going to . . . to . . ."

"Baby, let it happen. I'm only getting started."

She fell back against the pillows and Reese climbed onto the bed. He eased her thighs farther apart and then, hooking his thumbs in the sides of the thong, he shimmied it down her long legs and tossed it to the floor. He nibbled on the inside of her thigh, moving his mouth higher.

"Reese! You can't!"

He looked up at her desperate plea. "Hasn't anyone ever—"

"No! Not . . . like *that.*"

"Let me be the first." *The only,* he thought.

Halley looked down at his head between her thighs and shuddered. This was so intimate. He looked up at her, his eyes dark with passion. He was so sensual, so beautiful. There was nothing in her previous sexual experiences that came close to comparing with this.

"Trust, me. Relax."

She tried, but when she felt the petal-soft pressure of his mouth, the heat of his breath, the touch of his tongue, she tensed. This was too much.

"Let me love you."

His low plea made her muscles ease a bit. He kissed her . . . *down there,* moving his tongue in, slow and easy. She worried how she tasted, but just then he raised his head.

"You're sweet, like honey. I can't get enough. Are you ready?"

Ready? Dear God. Her answer was a whimper, a slight nod.

"Ahhh, good." He lowered his head, moving his tongue over her slick folds, up and down, harder, and then when her breath came in short gasps, he went faster. Wanton now, she arched up against his mouth, digging her fists into the covers, moving with him.

When he suddenly eased his hands underneath her ass and lifted, she cried out, "Reese . . . what . . . ?" She was open for him, glistening, swollen. He plunged his tongue in and out and just when she thought she couldn't stand the pleasure of it, he sucked on her clit. . . .

And she exploded. Delving her hands into his hair, she arched up off the bed and cried out. With a low chuckle, he lapped at her gently, making her shudder as wave after wave washed over her trembling body.

Drained, lethargic, she managed to raise her head and look at him. "That was . . . amazing." She realized he was still fully clothed and she was spread out before him like a banquet and it didn't seem fair. She suddenly felt the need for him to be naked. She pushed up on wobbly arms and tugged his shirt over his head. Her fingers found his belt buckle, but couldn't manage to unfasten it.

"Let me." He stood up and did the rest for her. She watched, mesmerized as he shucked his pants and then slipped out of his boxers. When he started to ease his big body onto the bed, she stopped him.

"Let me see you." Coming up to her knees, she let her hands skim over his wide shoulders, squeeze his powerful biceps. Tugging him forward, she let her tongue swirl over one flat nipple while her fingers trailed over his chest and down his ab muscles, which tightened and quivered beneath her hands. Then she hesitated. His erection bobbed near her mouth.

"You can touch and play. I'm all yours."

"I . . . I don't know how to please you that way."

He tucked a finger underneath her chin, tilting her

face up. "Halley, you'll please me no matter what you do." He smiled. "Just touch me."

She swallowed, licked her lips, and for a moment just looked her fill. Then she lightly ran her finger over the engorged head of his penis. When he inhaled sharply, she took the hard length of him in her hand. He pulsed with energy, strength. She couldn't imagine what it would feel like to have him inside her.

"Make love to me, Reese," she said softly. Putting her hands in his, she tugged him onto the bed.

"I need to put on protection. God, I hope I have a condom." Rolling to the side of the bed, he leaned over and found his pants, fumbled around in the pocket, and came up with one.

He joined her on his side, face to face, skin to skin. Moving seductively against her, he lightly ran one hand over her shoulder, down the curve of her belly. Easing her onto her back, he cupped her mound and slid one long finger inside her slick folds. She gasped.

"You're ready for me."

"Oh, yes." She looked into his eyes, knowing he'd love her like no other. "I'm yours," she said, and pulled his face to hers for a kiss. The touch of his lips to hers set her on fire. He kissed her deeply, devouring her mouth with an all-consuming kiss. Halley arched up, offering herself to him, wild with need.

"God, baby, you're tight." He eased into her inch by glorious inch and Halley was touched by his gentleness. Fully inside her, he moved slowly in and out and then said, "I'll go slow until you're ready."

God, he was so big, so powerful. She rubbed her hands over his back, loving the feel of the muscles flexing, bunching, as he thrust a little quicker. She knew he was holding back, but her orgasm was already building. She needed more. Thrusting her hips upward, she took him deeper, urged him faster.

He stretched her, filled her, made her blood sing.

"Ahh, Halley, come for me," he said low, sexily, in her ear. "You're so tight, so hot, so sweet. I could love you forever."

"Then do it. Love me forever." With a ragged cry, she arched her back, squeezed her legs around him, and met his deep thrusts until it was hard to tell where he began and she ended. The pleasure began building . . . and she climbed higher, reaching for the stars.

"Reese!" She clung to his powerful body, giving him everything she had, holding back nothing. When she was almost there, he slowed down, easing his hard length almost out of her, and then slowly back in. This made her frantic, wild for him. "Please," she panted, "more." He did it again, leaving her hanging on the edge, desperate for release. "No . . . I need . . ."

"This?" He angled her so he could hit the spot where she was on fire for him. He went fast, hard. Faster . . . *God*, deeper, until she cried out his name on the crest of an explosive climax. Still flying, she felt his whole body tense, and then he shuddered, holding her in a full-body embrace.

"My God," Halley breathed. Still clinging to him, loving the feel of him so deep in her womb, she kissed him tenderly. "You blow me away."

"I aim to please," he said with a weak chuckle, but his eyes were serious.

She wanted to tell him that it was more than the

sex. He had touched her on a deeper level. She barely knew Reese, but she knew one thing for certain. She never wanted to let him go. She smiled the languid smile of a woman well loved, and the thought hit her. . . . She had found her fantasy man, after all.

When he finally rolled to the side, Halley leaned up on one elbow to look at him. He returned her gaze through half-lidded eyes and gave her a heart-stopping smile. She traced his beautiful mouth with her fingertip, and then unable to resist, she leaned in and gave him a lingering kiss.

~ chapter
ten

He had never been the cuddling, kissing type, but he wanted to hold Halley in his arms all night long. He was good at sex, knew he would rock her out of her small-town world, but he hadn't expected the . . . *emotion*.

It was *his* world that had been rocked. He chuckled at the thought.

"What?" she asked lazily, still nibbling at his lips.

"I wanted to rock your world, and you, lady, turned the tables on me."

She giggled. "I like that. Makes me feel . . . invincible."

Reese ran his hand up the smooth skin of her leg and then, without warning, slipped his hand between her thighs. When his middle finger found her still sensitive clitoris, she gasped. "Reese . . ."

"I want to watch you come, Halley."

"Oh . . ." Her eyelids fluttered shut, and her head

fell back onto the pillow. His finger moved in a slow circle. It took only once, twice, and then her mouth parted, her breath hitched, and she arched up with a very long sigh. Rosy color blossomed in her cheeks, down her neck and chest.

"How . . . did I look?" she asked in a throaty voice, but kept her eyes shut.

"Beautiful." He kissed her lightly. "Absolutely beautiful." The thought suddenly occurred to him that if this was how his mother and father felt about each other, then no wonder they never gave a damn about how the world felt about them.

"You make me *feel* beautiful, Reese." She snuggled close and put her hand on his damp chest. Drawing small circles with her fingertip on his smooth skin, she said, "I've always been a tomboy. I've never been good at flirting or dating. But you've made me feel like, my God, so . . ."

"Sexy?"

"Umm-hmm."

Reese pushed up onto one elbow, facing her. "You *are* unbelievably sexy."

"I'm not curvy."

Reese cupped a breast, rubbed his thumb over the nipple, and smiled at her instant reaction. "You are more than enough, and the fact that you love sports, especially baseball, is even more of a turn-on."

She frowned. "I'm sure you're used to more—"

He silenced her by taking her breast in his mouth, teasing the beaded nipple with his tongue, and then sucking, hard, drawing another gasp. He soothed the nipple with several soft licks and then surprised her

with a sharp tug with his teeth that caused a quick intake of her breath and then a moan.

"I love your breasts," he said, and meant it. "I could
feast on them all night long." He looked at her with a
twinge of regret. "But I have to pitch tomorrow."

Her eyebrows shot up. "Ohmygod, is there some
kind of rule about sex the night before a game?"

Reese laughed, started to speak, and then laughed
again. He couldn't ever remember being so relaxed,
having so much fun with a woman.

Halley joined him. "Guess it's a moot point."

"No, sweetheart, there's no rule about sex before a
game, but if I stay here with you, I won't get an ounce
of sleep, and I think you know why." It surprised him
that he wanted to stay. In fact, it was going to be hard
to leave her. "Will you come watch me pitch?" He
asked the question without thinking, but found himself holding his breath waiting for her answer.

"You better believe it."

Reese felt a goofy leap of joy and he gave her a
quick kiss. "I'll leave a couple of tickets at the will-call
window."

"Thank you," she said, her voice muffled against his
chest. She sounded sleepy . . . sexy. Her cheek rested
against him while her hand leisurely rubbed back and
forth across his shoulder and then down his chest. She
snuggled closer, wrapping her leg over his hip.

Reese kissed her on top of her head. "Halley, I've
got to go."

She moaned a sleepy protest and looped her arm
around his neck. "Stay."

"Halley," he said gently. "You've already got me

hard as a rock. I want you all over again . . . and then again. Get the picture? Sex all night with you would be amazing, but I wouldn't be able to pitch worth a damn." He gently disentangled her long legs, but couldn't resist another long, hot kiss.

With a growl, he stood up and jammed on his boxers, but made the mistake of looking down at her. She was watching him with a hungry look. She blushed and caught her plump bottom lip between her teeth. Her dark hair, mussed in a glorious tangle against the white pillow, gave her a just loved look that had him clenching his fists in an effort not to lower his body back onto the bed and do her all over again.

"Please, just one more kiss good-bye." She raised her arms in invitation and something clenched in his gut.

Reese sat down on the bed, leaned in, and kissed her softly. "You make it hard for a guy to leave."

"I'm not being fair."

"I'm glad you bumped into me at Shakey's."

"Me too." She hesitated a moment as if she wanted to say more, but he put a finger to her lips. If she asked him to stay once more, he wouldn't have the will to leave.

"I'll see you tomorrow. We'll grab a bite to eat after the game, okay?"

She smiled. "Okay. I can't wait."

God. Reese fumbled with his clothes and somehow managed to leave. Once outside, he breathed the cool night air, strolled over to his SUV, and reluctantly headed home.

After arriving at his rented condo about twenty minutes later, Reese drank a cold beer and got ready for bed. He thought he would toss and turn with Halley on the brain, but he felt so relaxed, so content, that he almost immediately fell asleep.

Halley woke the next morning and stretched like a contented cat, but immediately realized that she was tender and sore in intimate places. She put a hand to her mouth when she remembered *how* she got that way. For a moment she closed her eyes, remembering . . . and almost jumped out of her skin when the phone rang. She reached over to the nightstand and picked up the receiver.

"Hello?"

"Hey, how's your ankle?" His voice was low and gravelly like he had just woken up. Halley imagined him in bed, sleep-rumpled, tangled in the sheet . . . and nothing else.

"I, uh, haven't tried it yet."

"Still in bed, sleepyhead?"

"Wanting you in it." She cringed. Where in the hell had that come from?

He chuckled. "Hey, you're learning to flirt."

She giggled.

"Ahh, now you're blushing. I can tell."

"That's because I'm imagining you naked." *What?*

"Hot damn." He laughed and she loved the sound of it. She made a mental note to make him do it more often.

Halley crossed her legs and leaned back against the pillows, enjoying herself. "So . . . *are* you?"

"Naked? No, but I can be. Are you?"

Halley peeked under the sheets. "Why, yes, I am."

"You're killing me. You know that, don't you?"

Halley laughed, feeling powerful in her newfound sexy skin. "I can't wait to see you pitch."

He groaned. "Now I'm nervous."

"How about this, then? I can't wait to have you in my arms."

He groaned again. "Now I'm—"

"Stop! Now you're killing *me*."

"Okay, off to another cold shower."

She giggled. "You took one already?"

"As soon as I thought about you."

"Now who is the flirt?" Halley twirled her finger in her hair while leaning against the pillows. She felt like a teenager talking to her boyfriend. When they finally ended the conversation fifteen minutes later, she felt absolutely giddy . . . and horny as hell.

Reese was on her mind at the goofiest of times for the rest of the afternoon. Things not remotely connected to him—TV commercials, a song on the radio, an airplane?—somehow reminded her of him.

Finally, it was time to get ready for the game. Since Reese had given her two tickets, she had asked Cole to go with her. Standing in her bedroom next to a mounting pile of clothes, Halley glanced over at her alarm clock as she changed into her fifth outfit.

"Damn, Cole is going to be here soon," she mumbled, deciding her jean shorts were too casual. Tossing them into her pile, she entered her closet and yanked a pair of black capri pants and a white halter top off the hangers.

"There," she said with a nod. The halter top had a

built-in bra, and showed more skin than she usually dared to. It had been a birthday gift from Sallie and she hadn't had the nerve to wear it, but today suddenly seemed like the day to bare her shoulders. The pants were slimming and casual with a chic flair that made her feel sexy. Black sandals and a matching purse, a silver chain and silver teardrop earrings, and she was ready for makeup.

Usually, she wore a little mascara and lipstick, but today, she added a little eyeliner and smoky eye shadow. She chose lip gloss that gave her a just kissed look that she hoped would drive Reese crazy.

The doorbell chimed. She added a spritz of perfume and hurried to the door.

Cole entered with a low whistle. "Whoa, baby sis. You look . . . hot."

"That's the look I'm going for."

Cole raised a dark eyebrow. "Are you on the prowl?"

Halley wrinkled her nose. "I don't *prowl*—that's your game. And I already have a date after the game with Reese Taylor."

His other eyebrow shot up and then scrunched into a frown. "Halley, you're asking for trouble."

Her eyes narrowed.

Cole held up his hands. "Hey, it's not the race thing, although you will get some flak over that, I'm certain." Cole put his hands on his lean hips. "I warned you that he's a hotshot. Goes through women faster than—"

"You?" Halley shook her head. "He's so different than he seems. Cole, there is a softer side that he keeps hidden beneath that bad-boy facade."

"It's not a facade." Cole let out a long sigh. "You're too damn trusting. I've seen Reese with at least a dozen women since I've been working with the Flyers. They hang out after the games waiting for him. Sis, you're setting yourself up for heartbreak."

Halley pursed her lips. "Spoken like the true heartbreaker that you are. By the way, stay away from Jenna."

"She asked me to Cathy's wedding."

"What! I hope you said no." She watched him rub his hand over the dark stubble shadowing his jaw. "You didn't!"

"I probably should have, but I promise to keep my lecherous hands to myself if it makes you feel any better."

Halley put her hands on her hips. "It does *not*."

Cole ran an impatient hand through his dark wavy hair. "I'm not going to hurt her, Halley, I—" He stopped and shook his head.

"You'll what?" Halley asked a little bit more gently. She remembered the look on his face after the kiss he shared with Jenna and it suddenly occurred to her that her playboy brother might actually care for her friend. That too, though, could spell trouble.

"Look, I'll take her to the damned wedding and that'll be it. Satisfied?"

Halley reached over and squeezed her brother's arm. "Hey, you know how much I love you, you big lug. Jenna is a wonderful girl. Maybe . . . just *maybe*, you should let down your eternal-bachelor guard and date her with the intention of starting a real relationship?"

His expression looked like he had just sucked on a lemon.

Halley threw up her hands. "It was just a passing thought." She swung her purse over her bare shoulder. "Okay, let's go watch some baseball."

Cole gave her a grin. "There's nothing better than baseball, hot dogs, and a cold beer."

"I think that's supposed to be apple pie."

"Not in my book."

She followed him out the door of her apartment. She was glad to drop the discussion, but she silently wished her brother would at least make a stab at a real relationship. Halley sometimes wondered if it was the death of their mother and watching their father's heartbreak at the loss that made Cole afraid to fall in love. She too had scoffed at the whole weak-kneed thing . . . until now. Perhaps perky little Jenna, with her enthusiasm for life and infectious smile, was just the woman to tame her big, bad brother.

"The tougher they are, the harder they fall," Halley said under her breath, realizing that that sentiment referred to her as well.

"You say something?" Cole asked as he eased his long legs into his sleek black Celica.

"Nothing. Just talking to myself. Step on it. I want to see batting practice."

"You got it."

Batting practice, my foot, she thought, and had to hide her grin. Reese Taylor in baseball pants was what she really wanted to see.

chapter eleven

"These are great seats," Cole commented when they sat down ten rows behind the backstop. "We're practically on the field."

"I love this stadium. It reminds me of Wrigley Field on a smaller scale. There's not a bad seat in the house, but you're right—these seats are awesome."

A vendor passed by lugging a cooler. "Ice-cold beer!" he boomed. "Get your ice-cold beer here."

"Don't have to twist my arm," Cole said, and signaled the gray-haired man over. He passed a beer to Halley. "Now all we need is a hot dog and I'm in heaven."

A moment later Cole had his hot dog slathered in mustard, but Halley was too nervous to eat. When Reese threw the first pitch of the game, her stomach did a little flip-flop. She took a long swallow of her beer, never taking her eyes from the action.

Ball one. She cringed when the next pitch was way

outside. Reese leaned forward with his forearm on his thigh, shaking off the sign from the catcher. Finally he nodded and threw a fastball down the center of the plate.

"Yes!" Halley exclaimed, letting out her breath. "Come on, Reese, strike this guy out."

He walked him, though, and the next batter as well. The crowd, rather large for a midweek game, grew noisy and restless. Halley wanted to stand up and shout for them to shut up and let him pitch, but gripped the arms of the metal chair and said a mental prayer instead.

"He's having control trouble," Cole commented. "He needs to settle down and get into a groove."

The next pitch looked good, but the ump called a ball, drawing a hiss from Halley. "That was a strike!"

"Looked good to me," Cole agreed.

The call seemed to agitate Reese. He stepped off the rubber and picked up the rosin bag, tossed it around in his left hand, and then went into his windup. The pitch was nothing but heat, right down the middle of the plate, followed by a curve that had the batter swinging and missing.

"Finish him off," Halley murmured.

Reese nodded to the catcher and went into his windup, firing what looked like a strike to Halley, but the umpire disagreed, causing her to do something she preached against in gym class. Shooting to her feet, she cupped her hands to her mouth and yelled, "Go get an eye exam, Blue! You stink."

Cole chuckled, drawing a glare from Halley. She plopped back down into the red metal seat hard enough to jar her teeth. If she weren't so pissed, she would be embarrassed, but right now, she wanted nothing more than to go nose to nose with the umpire. Gripping the arms of the chair, she held her breath, wondering how she was going to last nine innings.

"Fuck," Reese muttered, wiping sweat from his brow with the sleeve of his uniform. He had two men on base, no outs, and a full count. This was a hellava way to impress Halley. He shook off the sign for a curve, wanting to blow one right by this guy, knowing it was a risk. The curveball would be the safe thing to do. Feeling panic churn in his gut, he stepped off of the mound, picked up the rosin bag, and tossed it in his hand. He had decided to go with the curve even if it meant giving up a walk . . . and then he heard her above the buzz of the crowd.

"You can get this guy, Reese."

He glanced up into the crowd, something he never did, *shouldn't* ever do, and saw Halley on her feet. At that moment, the panic in his gut disappeared. Gritting his teeth, he stepped back onto the mound, went into his windup, and fired a fastball that sounded like a firecracker when it hit the catcher's glove.

"Stee-rike three!" the ump growled.

From that moment on, Reese found his groove, giving up only three hits the entire game, earning a win for the Flyers.

In the clubhouse, the team celebrated with jokes and the towel slapping on bare asses that Reese usually shied away from. Today, however his mood was soaring and he knew it had something to do with the win, and everything to do with Halley. When the team suggested wings and beer at Shakey's, Reese told them he would join them to celebrate.

Slinging his duffel bag over his shoulder, he left the clubhouse to meet Halley by his car, but then suddenly had doubts. Maybe Halley wasn't ready to be seen in public with him. Dinner at her house was one thing, but Reese didn't know how well he would deal with a racial remark from some drunken yahoo in a bar.

And then it hit him. He didn't fucking care. All that mattered was being with her, and to hell with what the rest of the world thought.

He spotted her sitting on a wooden bench in the courtyard near the parking lot. She smiled his way and waved, making him have the goofy urge to run over and pick her up, twirling her around while kissing her senseless.

She stood up and walked toward him looking sexy as hell in a halter top. Fighting the need to palm her breasts in his hands, he oh so politely leaned over and gave her a kiss on the cheek.

"You rocked out there today," she said, and held up her hand for a high five.

Reese laughed as he slapped her hand. "Do I get a chest bump too?"

"Of course." With a laugh, she gave a hard bump with her chest.

Damn. He snaked his hands around her waist and said in her ear, "Get in the car so I can kiss you without an audience." He unlocked the door and she slid into the seat. Rushing to the driver's side, he tossed his duffel into the backseat and then climbed into the SUV, thankful for the dark-tinted windows.

Pulling her from her seat onto his lap, he lowered his head and kissed her. He had meant for the kiss to be playful, but she moaned deep in her throat and he was lost. A slow burn started in his groin and spread like wildfire in his blood. He cupped her breast, rubbing his thumb over her hardened nipple through the silky material, wanting nothing more than to untie the knot at the nape of her neck and expose her breasts for his eyes, his mouth.

"Halley?" He nibbled on her neck, loving the sweet smell of her perfume.

"Hmm?"

"Baby, I wanted to take you to Shakey's with the team, but damn, I'm on fire for you."

"How about pizza in bed at my place?"

"Done."

The short ride back to her apartment seemed to take a lifetime, and with every passing minute Halley got hotter and hotter for him. Everything he did made it worse . . . the flex of his muscle when he turned the wheel, a heated look, and a sexy grin. By the time he swung his SUV into the parking space, she had her seat belt unhooked and her hand on the door handle.

They raced to her apartment, and she dropped her keys twice in a hurried attempt to unlock the door, before he took them from her and dropped them as well.

"In about two seconds, I'm plowing the door down with my shoulder," Reese growled. He tried once more, successfully, and they practically fell into the hallway, kissing, fumbling with clothes, laughing . . . moaning. Reese picked her up and took long-legged strides to her bedroom. He laid her on the mattress and began shucking his already half-removed clothing.

Halley watched him, wondering if it was possible to want a man more. Her heart pounded, her breath came in shallow gasps, and her whole body tingled with anticipation of having his smooth skin, hard body, next to hers.

"I want you naked." He eased his big frame onto the bed and untied the knot of her halter top, freeing her breasts.

His hot mouth, smooth, wet tongue, found her nipple, sending sharp sensation, sweet longing, all the way to the tips of her toes. Her head fell to the side as she leaned back on her hands, letting him lick and nibble. His hands found the side zipper of her pants and for a moment there was tugging, shifting, until she was naked.

She was so aroused that the instant Reese slipped his hand between her thighs she shuddered with an orgasm. Embarrassed, she hid her face against his chest.

"Hey, don't you dare hide from me," he said gently.

"God, you must think—"

"I think you're beautiful. I want you to come for me over and over." His hand lightly grazed over her skin, cupped a breast, making her shiver. "Don't be embarrassed—don't hold back. I'll do whatever you want me to do, and I want you to tell me exactly what that is."

"I can't."

"Sure you can." He turned, slipped on a condom, and waited.

"I . . . I want you to make love to me."

"How?"

"You know *how*, Reese."

"Baby, there are lots of ways. With my mouth?"

"No, with your . . . you know."

"This?" He placed her hand on his penis.

He was steely hard, hot. She rubbed her hand up the powerful length. "Yes."

"I want you on top so I can watch."

"H-how?"

"Like this." He propped himself up against the mound of pillows, half sitting up. "Straddle me."

Halley looked down at his jutting penis and imagined sinking down on him, inch by inch. "Mmm, okay." She lifted her leg over his waist, held on to his wide shoulders, and rose up to her knees. Easing down, she felt the tip of his penis enter her. Gasping, she said, "I have to go . . . slow. You're big . . . God."

He held her waist, guiding her, as she took more and more of his cock. So wet, so tight, so hot. He wanted to buck up and take her for a wild ride, but she needed time to adjust. Straddling him, she was so open. "Move with me, Halley." He eased her up and then slowly back in.

"Reese . . . mmm . . . you fill me up this way. God, I can feel you so far inside me." Leaning forward, she kissed him deeply while moving so slowly that it was driving him mad.

And then he realized that she knew it. "Halley!"

She shook her head. "I'm on top. I'm in control."

She lifted up to her knees and sank back down. "You feel sooo good." Leaning in close, she let her nipples graze his chest and then moved back so he could see her body connected to his. She ran her fingers over the muscles of his abs, slick now with a fine sheen of sweat.

And then she went faster. Moaning, he tightened his hands around her waist and set the pace even faster until he had her slapping her ass against him, taking all of him again and again. Her breasts jiggled. Her head tilted back. He felt the muscles in her thighs quiver.

Reese felt his orgasm building, climbing. "Come with me, baby," he pleaded. Reaching between their bodies, his finger probed in her damp nest of dark curls and found her clit, and he knew it would send her flying.

It did. When she cried out, he grabbed her and pumped into her, arching his hips, going deep with a mind-blowing climax.

She fell against him, and he wrapped his arms around her. It touched him that she was trembling, tenderly kissing his neck, his chin, and finally his mouth. Resting her forehead against his, she took a deep shuddering breath. "My heart is beating a million miles a minute."

At that moment, Reese knew he was falling in love. That thought should have made him jump up and run like hell, but instead, he felt a rush of warmth. Gently, he rubbed his hands up the graceful curve of her back. "You're a hellava woman, Halley Forrester," he said, and then chuckled. "That wasn't very poetic, was it?"

"Being a hellava woman suits me just fine." She

gave him a grin. "Now, how about some pizza, a cold beer, and ESPN?"

Reese leaned back against the pillows with his eyes closed. "Hot damn, I'm in heaven. Never thought I'd make it."

A little while later they were cuddled on the sofa eating hot veggie pizza washed down with beer in frosty mugs—another taste of heaven—while they watched major-league highlights. She didn't like the olives, so she picked them off of her pizza slice and fed them to him.

Reese felt comfortable, shirtless, barefoot, clad in his jeans, while she lounged in his red Flyers golf shirt. *I could get used to this*, he thought, and sighed.

"Tired?" she asked, looking over at him.

"A little."

"How's your arm?"

When had a woman ever asked him *that?* Never. "Like lead, but I'll recover. I didn't throw too many pitches tonight." He tried to stifle a yawn, not wanting to leave, but one escaped.

"You're exhausted," she chided, and took his empty pizza plate.

He yawned again. "I should go," he admitted, but made no move to get up.

Halley looked over at him. Bare-chested, he had his arms draped over the back of the floral sofa. His jeans were unsnapped, and partially unzipped, clearly revealing the fact that his boxers were lying somewhere on her bedroom floor.

Heat pooled in her belly and she gave him a slow

smile while pointing south. "Another part of your anatomy has other ideas."

Reese looked down at the head of his penis peeking up at her and laughed. "That part of me has a mind of its own when I'm anywhere near you."

"Well, then how about you come to bed and I'll take care of that part of you while you lie back and take it easy?"

Answering for him, his dick got instantly harder, boldly poking out of his jeans.

"I'm thinking that's a yes?" She tugged him up from the sofa without a protest. Leading him back to her bedroom, she wondered if she could fake knowing how to give a blowjob. *Does one learn as she goes? And what do you do with your teeth?*

Reese peeled out of his jeans and lay down on the bed. Gazing down at his big beautiful body, she had to wonder . . . *Where do you put all of that . . . man?*

chapter twelve

Reese could tell she had never gone down on a guy before and he found the knowledge rather endearing.

"You just relax . . . and enjoy," she said while frowning at his dick. She hesitated, and then decided to take off her clothes. Climbing onto the bed, she nudged his legs into a vee and then knelt between his knees. With her bottom lip caught between her teeth, she angled her head and then ran her hands up his thighs, shyly cupping his sac.

Propped against the pillows, Reese watched with one arm bent beneath his head, and decided that an inexperienced woman was much more erotic than a seasoned hummer giver. She seemed to take such delight in his body, another absolute turn-on. Her hands caressed his thighs, but then grazed past his penis, making him want to arch his back and say, "Hey, here it is." Instead, her hands moved over his chest, lingering on his pecs, and then over his abs. His muscles clenched and quivered.

"Relax, Reese," she said while bending at the waist to place wet kisses where her hands had just been . . . while ignoring where he needed her most. Her hair trailed over his skin, tickling and teasing, while her hot little mouth kissed and licked everywhere except for his damned dick.

"Halley!"

"Shhh," she soothed, causing a rush of warm breath to caress his cock. And then the very tip of her tongue touched the head of his penis, making him practically levitate off of the mattress. Before he could recover, she had him in her mouth, caressing, loving, and giving. Entwining her fingers with his, Halley was turning him inside out with her tender assault, slowly bringing him to the brink, until he exploded with a climax that came from deep within.

Afterward, she snuggled next to him, her head on his shoulder, and her hand on his chest. "Stay with me," she said softly.

Reese Taylor didn't trust his voice, so he answered by hugging her close to his body. He had absolutely no intention of leaving.

The next morning he awoke to the aroma of bacon and coffee. Stretching his arms over his head, he wondered if there was any end to the wonderfulness of this woman. A moment later she walked into the room with a steaming mug of coffee in her hand, and he smiled, thinking, *Apparently not.*

"I didn't know how you like it, so I added just a bit of cream and sugar."

Reese scooted up in bed and accepted the mug. "Perfect."

She seemed delighted. "Really? I guessed right?"

Reese patted the mattress and she sat down. "You did, but I doubt if there is anything you could do that wouldn't please me."

She gave him such a sweet smile that his heart skipped a beat. Her hair was damp and fragrant from a shower and she wore no makeup, giving her a fresh look that totally did him in. A short robe gaped at the thigh and he couldn't resist running his hand over her smooth skin.

"Oh, no, you don't." She playfully slapped at his hand. "Breakfast is ready."

"Can't I have *you* for breakfast?"

She giggled. "No, you need a big hearty breakfast to give you lots of energy."

"Ah, now you're talkin'."

"How do you like your eggs?"

"Scrambled."

"Good, me too. I'll see you in the kitchen."

"Care if I take a shower?"

"Make it a quick one," she said over her shoulder. "I'm hungry."

Reese swung his legs over the bed and hurried to the bathroom. A few moments later, he was soaping his body under the hot spray . . . and found himself *singing* . . . and he was *not* a singing-in-the-shower kinda guy. Hell, he didn't sing, period.

But today, he felt like singing.

* * *

Halley whisked the eggs, put English muffins in the toaster, and then went to the fridge in search of butter and strawberry jam. After putting those items on the small kitchen table, she looked up to find Reese watching her. He stood with his shoulder propped against the doorframe and wore nothing but his faded jeans and a sexy grin. Morning stubble made him look incredibly masculine.

Unable to resist, she walked slowly toward him, reached up, and ran her hand over his sandpaper cheek. He angled his cheek into her palm, and his eyes closed. Halley reached up with her other hand and kissed him. "You taste minty fresh."

"I found a new toothbrush. I hope you don't mind."

"Not at all." She wanted to tell him that he could leave the toothbrush there for future use, but didn't have the nerve. She didn't want to be one of those clingy women who drove men away early in a relationship. With a gesture toward the table, she said, "Have a seat and I'll scramble the eggs." It occurred to her that in her twenty-four years, she had never cooked breakfast for a man other than Cole and her father . . . and she liked it. She enjoyed fussing around, filling his coffee cup, and eating with him.

When the English muffins popped up, he got up and snagged them from the toaster and then held the plates while she scooped eggs from the skillet.

Reese sat down and took a bite of eggs. "Delicious."

"Thanks. Breakfast is my favorite meal."

They ate in companionable silence for a while and

Halley was surprised how comfortable she felt sitting next to him at her kitchen table.

"Would you like to go to the game again tonight?" Reese asked. "It starts at seven and I'll take you to dinner afterwards."

"I can't. I have a final fitting for my bridesmaid's dress for Cathy's wedding."

Reese nodded. "Oh, the one from the bachelorette party at Shakey's?"

"Yes. She teaches at Sander's High with me. We've been friends for a long time." Halley nibbled on the inside of her lip for a moment, trying to decide if her next offer would be too bold. . . .

Reese reached across the table, picked up her hand, and rubbed the inside of her palm. "Whatever is going on in that pretty little head of yours, I want to know."

"Well . . . I could give you a set of keys to my place and you could come on over after the game and let yourself in, since I'm not sure when I'll be finished. I shouldn't be too terribly late," Halley said, hoping she didn't sound too needy.

Reese smiled, bringing her hand to his mouth for a kiss. "I can do that. I'll grab a bite after the game—be ready with the popcorn when you arrive."

"Good," she said, and found an extra set of keys for him in her junk drawer.

Reese pocketed the keys and then helped her clear the table. "I have to go," he said when they were finished. "We've got a meeting at the clubhouse at noon."

"I'll see you tonight, then," she said, and wanted to

machine. The thought of Halley chuckling over the message was just too damn hard to bear.

When he got to his SUV, he realized he still had the water bottle in his hand. He drained it, then tossed it in a nearby dumpster and headed for his condo. On his way home, though, he found himself pulling into Shakey's, knowing full well that in his state of mind, he should continue home. Something, though, compelled him to head inside with the chip on his shoulder throbbing.

A couple of teammates called his name. Reese waved, but headed straight for the bar and ordered a beer. Tilting the cold brown bottle to his lips, he saw the blonde heading his way. His first thought was to resist, but Halley's face flitted through his brain and he suddenly wanted to erase the hurt, maybe prove to himself she didn't matter, so he gave the blonde an I-want-to-fuck-you smile.

She gave it right back. "Hey there, handsome. You want to dance?"

Reese hated dancing, but he saw Cole Forrester glaring at him out of the corner of his eye and answered, "Yeah, sure." At that moment, he was spoiling for a fight or maybe just wanted Cole to tell Halley what a bastard he was. Maybe both.

"My name's Crystal," she cooed in his ear.

"Reese."

"I know. You're that ballplayer." She swayed next to him, dancing suggestively with her arms up over her head and her tits rubbing against his chest.

Her slutty act left him cold and he wanted nothing

more than for the song to end. Coming here had been a mistake. She ground her hips against him, snaked her arms around his neck, and before he could back away had her damned beer-soaked tongue in his mouth.

Reese pulled his mouth from hers, but she didn't get the hint and started nibbling on his ear and then, *Jesus*, stuck her tongue in, gagging him.

"I wanna fuck you," she slurred.

Reese moaned, giving her the wrong impression.

She leaned in to kiss him again, but thankfully the song ended.

"Meet me out back," Reese said in her ear.

She nodded and squeezed his ass. "Sure, baby. I need to make a pit stop in the ladies' room for a condom. I just bet you need an extra large."

"How'd you guess?" Reese asked dryly.

"I've heard that black men are huge."

"You are so right. I'll see you in a few minutes with my big black dick ready."

She turned and almost ran to the ladies' room while Reese headed to the front door. Once outside, he took a deep breath of fresh air, trying to get her stale scent out of his lungs.

"What the fuck do you think you're doing?"

Reese whirled around to face Cole Forrester. "Heading out, not that it's any of your damned business."

"I thought you were dating my sister."

"Your sister got what she wanted."

"You son of a bitch."

Reese saw the fist coming but didn't bother to duck. The impact of the blow to his jaw and another to his gut had him stumbling backwards into the brick wall.

Cole fisted his hand in Reese's shirt and glared at him. "I warned her about you, but she wouldn't listen."

Reese chuckled darkly. "Is that right?" He tasted blood with the tip of his tongue. "Well, somebody should have warned me that she just wanted to get laid by a black man." He dodged the uppercut and pushed Cole. "I was just some wager in a damned bachelorette party game." He gave Cole another hard shove. "Now get the fuck out of my way."

Cole backed up a step and his glare softened as if he knew what Reese was talking about. "Halley's not that way. Listen, that was just a stupid game. It didn't mean anything."

"I get that part."

"No, wait—"

"Get out of my way, Cole," Reese said tiredly. "Chase Mitchell will suspend me if I get into a fight. And I need to make it to the majors so I can get the hell out of this town."

Cole looked like he wanted to say more, but backed away. With a weary sigh, Reese headed for home.

❧ chapter
thirteen

Halley frowned when she didn't see Reese's black SUV in the parking lot. She hurried to her apartment and was disappointed to find him not there. When a glance at the answering machine showed that she had no new messages, a weird feeling in the pit of her stomach told her that something was wrong.

She put a hand to her mouth. "God, what if he's been in an accident?" Her heart pounded and she reached for the phone, dialing his number, which she had written on a note held to the fridge with a magnet.

When his answering machine picked up, she left a message. "Reese, this is Halley. Is everything all right? Please call when you get this message. Oh, and there is something I keep forgetting to ask you . . . so call, okay?" Nibbling on the inside of her lip, she hung up. Something wasn't right. She could feel it.

Still frowning, she opened the refrigerator and was

grabbing a bottle of water when the doorbell rang. With a smile, she hurried over to open the door and was surprised to see her brother.

"Cole?" She shut the door after he entered. "What's up?"

"I screwed up."

"What?"

"Okay, stay calm."

"You're scaring me."

"I had a fight with Reese."

"What!" She took a step toward him. "You mean, like, you *hit* him?"

"A couple of times."

"What?"

"Quit saying *what*, and just listen to me for a second."

"Is that why he's not here?"

Cole grabbed her by the shoulders. "Listen! He somehow found out about that screwy fantasy man bullshit you girls were doing at the bachelorette party."

"How?"

Cole headed to the kitchen for a beer. Snagging one from the fridge, he shrugged. "I don't know. But he thinks you were out for a piece of black ass and nothing more."

Halley felt heat creep into her cheeks.

"You sleeping with this guy, Halley?"

"It's much deeper than that. Cole, I've never felt like this before. I thought all that weak-kneed, butterflies-in-the-stomach stuff was a bunch of bull."

"It is."

Halley shook her head and then stared up at her brother. "Do you think I'm in love?"

Cole choked on a swallow of beer. "You're asking me?"

"Point taken. Cole . . . what am I going to do?"

"If it were me, I'd cut my losses and move on."

Halley felt a tear roll down her cheek.

"Okay, you're not me," he tried to joke. "Sis, go see him."

"What if he won't let me in, or listen to reason?"

"I'll kick his ass."

Halley came up on her toes and poked a finger at his chest. "Touch him again and I'll kick *your* ass."

"Hot damn. I think you *are* in love."

Halley shook her head and sniffed loudly. "Yeah. I think I am. Now if I can only convince him."

Cole grinned. "Oh, I think you can."

Reese toweled off after a long hot shower to wash away the smell of beer, cheap perfume, and cigarette smoke. Circling away the fog in the bathroom mirror, he examined his busted lip and bruised ribs where Cole had landed a nasty jab. The only reason he hadn't punched Cole back was because he had been defending his sister . . . and that sister happened to be Halley.

Damn, the mere thought of her had him getting hard. And that pissed him off. Reese closed his eyes and leaned against the cold porcelain sink. For a moment there, he'd thought he had found something special, something lasting. But it was all just part of a stupid game.

With a deep sigh that made his bruised ribs hurt, he

tucked the towel around his waist and headed to his closet for some flannel lounging pants. He had just tugged them on when he heard the doorbell chime. Still tying the drawstring, he headed down the stairs, but then hesitated before opening the door. It was late, almost eleven. Who could it be? The trashy blond woman from the bar wanting to get laid? Cole to kick his ass again?

His heart hammered in his chest. *Halley?*

He stood there with his hand on the doorknob and then realized he was being a complete pussy. Swallowing, he put a classic Reese Taylor scowl on his face and swung open the door.

Shit, she was crying. Not a noisy, whiny sobbing. Just tears running down her face.

"May I come in?" Her voice was husky, shaky.

Reese tried hard not to be moved, not to drag her into his arms. Instead, he gave a curt nod and stepped back to let her enter. Folding his arms across his chest, he leaned against the wall, gave her a level look, and waited.

Her chin trembled, but she opened her mouth to speak and then her watery blue eyes widened. "My God, your lip is busted, and oh, you're bruised." She took a step closer and, reaching a hand toward his face, touched his swollen lip. A fat tear rolled down her face. "I'm sorry."

Reese would have stepped away, but was trapped by the wall. Her gentle touch caused an ache, a longing that pissed him off when he remembered that he was just a fling for a bored, small-town teacher. "Believe me, this is nothing. So if you came to apologize—"

"I came to explain."

"The situation is pretty black-and-white, if you'll pardon the pun. You needed me for your little fantasy game and I gave you what you wanted. Glad to have been of service." He pointed to the door. "Now you can go."

"Screw the black-and-white thing, and I'm not going anywhere. Don't you see the irony of the whole damned situation?"

"No."

She raised her palms upward. "You *are* my fantasy!" She took a step toward him and this time her touch wasn't gentle. She poked him in the chest. "That's right! Not only do you make me melt with just a look, but we enjoy the same things. Damn it, I never felt this way about anyone, and if I met you because of a silly *fucking* game then just"—she pointed a finger again to emphasize—"get *over* it!" Then she turned beet red and put a hand over her mouth.

Reese blinked at her for a long moment while she held her breath. "Why, Miss Forrester. I do believe you need a spanking for that nasty language."

When she moaned and hid her red face with her hands, Reese reached over and gently pried them away. "Come here." He tugged on her wrists.

She blinked up at him, unsure.

"Halley, I don't want to be your fantasy."

Her gaze dropped to the floor. "Oh."

He put a fingertip underneath her chin, forcing her to look at him. "I want to be your reality."

She leaned against him, wrapped her arms around

his neck, and gently kissed the corner of his mouth, avoiding his busted lip.

Reese could taste the salt of her tears mixed with the sweet heat of her mouth. He pulled back from her and wiped away her tears with his thumbs. "Baby, don't cry. You're tearing me up." Tugging her hands, he pulled her toward the steps leading to his bedroom. She stumbled against him. "Is your ankle still sore?"

"No, it's that annoying weak-kneed thing that happens when you kiss me."

He scooped her up into his arms. "I can do more than make your knees weak."

With her arms linked around his neck, she smiled at him. "Tell me something I *don't* know."

"I'm falling in love with you." He hadn't expected to say it, but the admission made him feel . . . *euphoric*. Stupid happy.

"Ohmygod." She hugged him so hard that he lost his balance and fell onto the bed. "Ohmygod." She landed on top of him, crying, laughing, and placing wet kisses all over his face.

Reese laughed. She finally sat up, straddling him.

"And I'm falling head over heels for you, Reese Taylor." Her blue eyes, shiny from her tears, were serious.

Reese reached up and cupped her cheek with his hand, wiping away her tears. "Halley, being with me won't be easy. If I get called up—"

"*When* you get called up."

He smiled, but then turned serious as well. "I could get traded, have to move. I travel all the time. And the race thing will always be there to deal with. No matter how much it *shouldn't* matter . . . it still does."

"That's reality, Reese. You said you wanted to be my reality, not my fantasy. I can deal with it." She gave him a determined lift of her chin and tried to look tough, but she was such a sweetheart. . . .

And she was sitting on top of him, in his bed.

"Halley?"

"Hmm?"

"A little fantasy might be a good thing. Any ideas?"

"Let's see." With her bottom lip caught between her teeth, she traced her finger over his chest and then slowly untied the drawstring of his pants. "How about if we pretend that you're a gorgeous, hotshot baseball player and I'm a shy, small-town teacher, and we fall in love and have *hot*, steamy sex."

"But Halley, that's reality."

She looked up from the trail of kisses she was placing on his chest that were heading south. "Exactly. And it's all I want, all I'll ever need."

"Come here," he said, his voice gruff with emotion. He wrapped his hands around her waist and scooted her up for a long, hot kiss. He wanted to make love to her, but for the moment was content to hold her in his arms. "My mother is going to adore you," he said, kissing her on top of the head. His comment was spontaneous, from the heart, but when he saw the surprised smile on her face, he was glad he had voiced his thoughts out loud.

"Really?" she asked softly. "You think so?"

"I know so."

"When will I get to meet your parents?"

"They're flying in from California next week to take in a few games."

"Well, then, I get to show you off at Cathy's wedding this Saturday. I've been meaning to ask you for days. Will you go with me?"

"Are you kidding? I don't even want to think about other guys slow dancing with you. Of course, I'll go with you."

"My god," Halley breathed as she scooted back up, leaned in and kissed him. "It must be happening." She giggled as she leaned over and entwined her fingers with his.

"What are you talking about?" Reese looked up at her with an amused frown.

"I told Jenna that the day I fell in love and found a guy who could make me go weak in the knees, pigs would fly." She moved seductively against him and smiled. "Somewhere, there is a pig who has just sprouted wings."

about
the author

LuAnn McLane lives in Florence, Kentucky. When she isn't
writing, she enjoys long walks with her husband, chick flicks
with her daughter, and tries to keep up with her three
active sons. She loves hearing from her readers. You can
reach her at luann@excessstreet.com or visit her Web site,
www.luannmclane.com.

water from the fridge, hoping she would arrive soon. The phone rang, but he was in midswallow and the answering machine picked it up.

A sultry female voice with a hint of the South began talking. "Oh, damn, Halley, I meant to dial your cell. I got stuck late at the shop. Anyway, hey, I heard it through the grapevine that you're seeing that hunk of man Reese Taylor. Ooowee. I want details. I guess you found your fantasy black man in our little bachelorette wager. Too smooth the way you snagged him at the bar. Didn't know you had it in you. You win, girlfriend. Half price on anything in my shop is yours. And I want some delicious details, you hear me?"

For a long moment, Reese stood perfectly still in the center of the kitchen, blinking at the answering machine. Frowning, he shut his eyes and tried to remember details of the night he met her at Shakey's. So Halley bumping into him at the bar hadn't been an act of fate. She had planned it. He had been a fucking wager. A black man? Her mission that night was to snag a black man? He just happened to be available and all too willing.

Reese felt anger bubble up inside. No, this was worse than anger. . . . Reese swallowed the tightness in his throat. This *hurt*. Gripping the water bottle tightly, he had the almost uncontrollable urge to throw it against the wall. He took a deep breath, trying to calm himself down. "I gotta get out of here," he mumbled, hoping Halley didn't arrive before he was gone. But before he walked out the door, he deleted the message from the ask him to the wedding, but the phone rang before she had the chance.

"I'll get my stuff and let myself out," he said, and gave her a kiss on the cheek as she was picking up the receiver.

The call was from Cathy, reminding her about the fitting. They chatted about the wedding for a while, but Halley's mind was really on Reese, and what the night would bring.

"You pitched a great game last night, Reese," Chase Mitchell commented after the game. "I was impressed with how you kept your cool when you got into a jam early on." He slapped Reese on the back. "Keep it up and I'll lose you to the big dance."

"Thanks," Reese said as he shoved his gear into the locker. Chase wasn't one to give out undeserved praise, so Reese knew he meant what he said.

Reese hung around long enough to have a beer with the team, but when a poker game broke out, he begged off and left, eager to get to Halley's. On the way, he went through a drive-through and picked up a burger and fries, polishing them off just as he arrived at her complex.

It felt weird letting himself into her apartment, but just being in her place gave him a sexual charge. The scent of her perfume hung in the air along with other reminders of her personality. He ran a finger over an antique chest and grinned when he picked up a framed snapshot of her spiking a volleyball over the net in a Sander's High uniform.

Flipping on the kitchen light, he grabbed a bottle of